Ree saw the vehicle barreling toward them...

Quint pulled out a Glock at the same time Ree pulled hers. Cell phone in one hand, she tried to snap a picture of the license plate of the black Acura gunning for them.

"I'll swerve as he gets close, blocking the road. You bolt out the passenger side and get to our witness's family," Quint said. All this would be for nothing if they couldn't save Ivan's wife and daughter. He would clam up faster than a metal trap stepped on by a bear.

"Let's do this," Ree said.

Quint stomped the brake, causing the truck to slant sideways before screeching to a halt. The second it slowed down, Ree made a run for it.

Gunfire caused her to duck, then run in a zigzag to make herself a more difficult target. Cell phone in hand, Ree fired off a text to their standby Bureau contact. The only word she needed to send was *help...*

EYEWITNESS MAN AND WIFE

USA TODAY **Bestselling Author**

BARB HAN

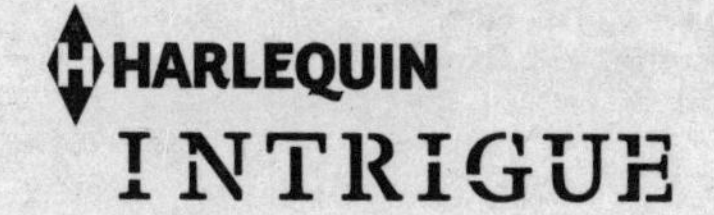

All my love to Brandon, Jacob and Tori,
the three great loves of my life.

To Babe, my hero, for being my best friend,
greatest love and my place to call home.

I love you all with everything that I am.

Recycling programs for this product may not exist in your area.

ISBN-13: 978-1-335-58200-3

Eyewitness Man and Wife

For questions and comments about the quality of this book, please contact us at CustomerService@Harlequin.com.

Harlequin Enterprises ULC
22 Adelaide St. West, 41st Floor
Toronto, Ontario M5H 4E3, Canada
www.Harlequin.com

Printed in U.S.A.

USA TODAY bestselling author **Barb Han** lives in north Texas with her very own hero-worthy husband, three beautiful children, a spunky golden retriever/standard poodle mix and too many books in her to-read pile. In her downtime, she plays video games and spends much of her time on or around a basketball court. She loves interacting with readers and is grateful for their support. You can reach her at barbhan.com.

Books by Barb Han

Harlequin Intrigue

A Ree and Quint Novel

Undercover Couple
Newlywed Assignment
Eyewitness Man and Wife

An O'Connor Family Mystery

Texas Kidnapping
Texas Target
Texas Law
Texas Baby Conspiracy
Texas Stalker
Texas Abduction

Rushing Creek Crime Spree

Cornered at Christmas
Ransom at Christmas
Ambushed at Christmas
What She Did
What She Knew
What She Saw

Decoding a Criminal

Visit the Author Profile page at Harlequin.com.

CAST OF CHARACTERS

Emmaline Ree Sheppard, aka Ree—This ATF agent will do anything to protect a partner who refuses to save himself.

Quinton Casey, aka Quint—This hotshot ATF agent blames himself for the death of his pregnant partner, Tessa, and will stop at nothing to put the person responsible behind bars, which endangers himself in the process.

Axel Ivan—Set up for a prison-yard murder, he just might offer the key to the investigation.

Giselle Langley—This mistress leads the investigation to Dumitru's right hand, but is she truly what she appears to be?

Vadik Gajov—This ruthless criminal is the right hand of crime boss Dumitru.

Dumitru—The ultimate target and person responsible for Tessa's murder is elusive—too much so?

Chapter One

Agent Quinton Casey stood on the porch of the two-bedroom bungalow with his fist raised and ready to knock. This visit was supposed to be him showing up with a suitcase in hand, ready to personally measure Ree Sheppard's bed to see if it was big enough to fit him and her together. The invitation to try a sleepover unrelated to their jobs as undercover ATF agents—they'd been partners on the last two cases—wasn't something Quint had intended on wasting. Halfway down the Texas highway in between Fairfield and Madisonville, things had changed when he got a call from Agent Grappell, the desk agent who had been assigned to their previous cases. Now, Quint had to deliver the news that the person they'd arrested a couple of days ago had been killed in jail, along with any hope they would be able to get a name from him or a trail to follow like they'd hoped.

Quint lowered his elbow and put his hand on his hip instead. The direct link to a crime ring responsible for killing his best friend and fellow agent was gone forever.

Raising his fist once again to knock, the door swung open. Emmaline Ree Sheppard stood there with a confused look on her face. His lips still sizzled from the heat in their last kiss, but he couldn't let himself think about that right now.

"Are you going to stand here all day or decide to knock?" Ree asked. She crossed her arms over her chest, shifted her weight to one side, and chewed on the inside of her cheek as she studied him. She glanced at his hands, no doubt noticing the lack of suitcase. "What is it? What's wrong, Quint? Because if this is about you letting me down easy or telling me there will be no sleepovers, you didn't need to drive all the way out here to do th—"

"Constantin is dead." Ever since hearing the news, Quint had felt lost.

"What? How did this happen? He was in solitary confinement," she said, bringing her hand up to cover her mouth, all color drained from her face. She'd been there alongside him in Houston for the undercover sting that had ended with Constantin in handcuffs and the promise he would talk for a more lenient sentence. She clearly realized the trail to finding and locking up Tessa's killer had dried up once again. All the work done on the last two undercover cases that had led to this bust had gone up in smoke.

"Prisoners get an hour a day outside in the yard. It's supposed to be alone, but the guards said there was a paperwork error and he ended up with the regular population," Quint informed her, clenching his back teeth in a failed attempt to bite back some of his anger. He knew full well a guard had to have been paid off for a prisoner to be strangled to death in the yard. This also brought him back to the men who'd been arrested the night Tessa was shot. A-12 was the group he and Tessa had spent weeks cracking. They'd gotten in, but since drugs were involved the DEA showed up on bust day. Politics had been involved, since there were political ties to the case, and the governor needed a win against crime. Everything about the case got complicated. They busted five guys, but Quint always felt it was the tip of the iceberg. One of his informants gave him the name Dumitru as the head of the A-12 crime ring before the bust went down. Once the dust settled and he checked back, no one arrested went by that name. All five of the others, however, died in prison within two weeks of each other—two suspected suicides, and two had been outright killed. The last guy was put in solitary confinement for his own protection, but he was poisoned.

And now Constantin was dead.

"This is bad, Quint." Ree opened the door a little more before turning around and walking away. He'd noticed that she'd glanced at his empty hand twice and decided this wasn't the time to tell her that he'd left his suitcase in the car. The whole point of bringing it in the first place was to see what might happen if they were together for personal reasons.

He closed the door behind him before walking to

the small dining table next to the kitchen, where she was putting on a pot of coffee. He'd left his case folder in the vehicle, too. It was never far despite the fact this was supposed to be a social visit.

"A guard 'found' him about an hour and a half ago facedown in the grassy area behind the basketball post, strangled to death," Quint explained, smacking his flat palm on the small table. "What the hell am I supposed to do now?" Every person who could have helped him get to the person responsible for Tessa's death had ended up dead.

"We'll find another trail," Ree said, pouring fresh coffee in a pair of mugs. She handed one over, then took a sip from her own. "Give it some time."

Quint issued a sharp sigh.

"I do realize patience isn't your finest asset," she said with a smile that caused a little bit of the ice encasing his heart to chip away. This visit was supposed to have gone a whole lot differently than this and should have ended up with the two of them tangled in the sheets. He wanted nothing more than to get lost with Ree, if only for a couple of hours. But it would be a temporary break. The demons would return and he would be right back to this same spot of anger and frustration. "I always thought it was your eyes."

"Keep saying stuff like that and I'll be forced to lean across this table and kiss you," he said. The round table was small for a person of his considerable size. At six feet three inches he'd never be accused of being short.

Closing the distance between them wouldn't take much in the way of effort.

"What's stopping you?" she asked. It was a distraction, but it was also working.

"Your wish is my command." He leaned over and pressed his lips to hers, releasing a little of the pent-up frustration burning him from the inside out. There was something about Ree that helped him remain calm, no matter how irritated he got with a case. She had a soothing presence underneath that fiery red hair of hers that reminded him of all things fall, his favorite time of year. Those auburn locks fell well past her shoulders and brought out the emerald green in her eyes—eyes that were shielded by the thickest, blackest lashes he'd ever seen. Those eyes had a piercing quality that made him relieved he wasn't sitting on the opposite side of an interrogation table from her. She would see right through lies and into the depths of a person's soul.

After pulling back from the kiss, he rested his forehead against hers. Memories of the line they'd crossed on their last case flooded him. Having sex was supposed to tamp down some of the ache he felt whenever she was in the same room. Instead, it only made him want to be with her even more. *Great job there, Quint.*

"I did bring it," he said, referring to the suitcase.

"I know," she said without missing a beat.

"Then why did you give me 'the look' at the door?" he asked, leaning back in his seat and grabbing his coffee mug. He needed a caffeine boost to clear his thoughts.

"Because you didn't have it in your hand, which meant you had second thoughts." She picked up her coffee mug and stared inside.

"About us taking our relationship to the next level? Never," he confided. "The timing? There's where the doubts come in."

"Working together is a problem if we're going to date," she agreed, her lips compressing into a frown.

"Right now, I need you as my partner," he said. "I can't risk you asking to be reassigned because our chemistry fizzles."

"Is that what you think is going to happen?" Ree stood up and crossed into the kitchen like she needed to put space between them. She didn't stop until she was at the farthest point from him, and she rolled the coffee mug in between her palms, fuming. It seemed to be taking great effort for her not to speak her mind.

Quint's cell buzzed, interrupting the moment, and he couldn't decide if it was a good thing or not.

"Hold that thought?" he asked as he fished the phone out of his front pocket.

Ree gave a slight nod. Not a great sign but at least she was still willing to talk to him. The fizzle comment had sounded so much better inside his head. It never should have slipped through his filter and come out in a way that put whatever was happening between them in a bad light. But he also couldn't give her what she deserved until he put the bastard who'd been responsible for Tessa's death behind bars. An annoying voice in the back of his head picked that moment to ask if locking up Dumitru would be enough. It wouldn't bring back Tessa or her unborn baby.

"It's Agent Grappell," he said, checking the screen before answering.

"I have good news," Grappell said. Working weekends came with the territory of an undercover agent, but Grappell always went above and beyond the call of a desk agent. "Well, not exactly good but better."

"Okay. Mind if I put you on speaker?" Quint asked. "Ree's in the room."

"She is?" Grappell didn't hide his surprise. Considering it was the weekend and their last case was closed, there wasn't an official reason for the two of them to be together. Quint's personal life wasn't up for discussion. For all Grappell knew, Quint could have shown up to tell Ree the news about Constantin in person.

"Yes," Quint confirmed.

"Of course. Put her on the line."

Quint tapped the screen and motioned for Ree to come closer. She stood her ground in the kitchen and shot him the look that said she was in no mood. He realized in that moment just how big his mistake with her had been.

REE COULD LISTEN just fine from where she stood in the kitchen, tapping her toe. The word *fizzle* would forever be on the list of words she never wanted to hear again in any context. Right now, it needed to go on the back burner so she could focus on what Agent Grappell had to say.

"We have a name of the prisoner who is being held responsible for Constantin's death," Grappell said after perfunctory greetings. "Of course, the warden said he is conducting a full investigation. However, Bjorn was able to pressure him into providing details since they pertain to our ongoing investigation."

A few thoughts ran through Ree's mind. Was this person aware of whom he'd killed? Another thought—did he really care? Was he a patsy? Was he given a pack of cigarettes and extra privileges to take out the new prisoner?

"And?" Quint asked. The rim of his coffee cup suddenly became very interesting. She didn't need to look him in the eyes to realize he would have those same questions.

"You've been granted permission to interview him," Grappell said.

Quint lifted his gaze toward her, but Ree turned to look out the kitchen window.

"You'd have a voice box, of course," Grappell continued. A voice box would distort their voices so they wouldn't be identifiable later to the person being interviewed or anyone else around. "And you'd be able to see him, but he'd be looking at a two-way mirror."

The usual protocol would be in place.

"Why would this guy tell us anything?" Ree asked.

"If he's convicted, he would be facing the chair. Says he'll be killed long before then and it'll be made to look like a suicide. All the guy says he wants is to live long enough for his daughter to graduate high school in four years. She's a freshman," Grappell informed them.

"Strange request from an inmate who just committed murder," Ree said.

"The guy says he had no choice," Grappell said.

"Isn't that what they all say?" Ree quipped.

"He wants a transfer to a prison closer to his wife and daughter, too," Grappell continued. "Said if he gives up names, he'll have a target on his back if he isn't moved."

"What's he in for?" Quint asked.

"Weapons charges," Grappell said. "The arresting officer in this case was almost one-hundred-percent certain this guy was covering for someone else when he was busted."

"He was willing to take a fall for someone in A-12?" Quint asked. Ree already knew the crime ring was notorious for running guns and had been difficult to pin down because they trusted few people, kept their operation slim and efficient, and the few people on the lower rungs of the ladder had to be willing to take a fall when necessary. It was part of their code. The business was lucrative for those who were able to make the commitment.

"He was in A-12," Grappell stated.

"Why would he turn on them now?" Quint asked.

"First of all, he already gave a statement denying involvement with the death of the new inmate. He said a guard did and that he can prove it. He was a witness to the crime," Grappell continued.

"Is he threatening with a lawyer?" Quint asked.

"No, not yet anyway," Grappell stated.

"I'm confused. Why would he go against a major crime ring with the power to kill someone on the inside who is supposed to be in solitary confinement?" Ree asked. "It doesn't make sense."

"He says his wife and kid are in danger and need to go into Witness Protection immediately," Grappell stated. "Someone will come for them the minute word leaks that he's talking or being moved. He begged for protection for his family. Said we could lock him up for the rest of his life and throw away the key, but please keep his family safe. He finished by saying once he was gone they would come for his family."

"What did Bjorn say?" Quint asked. Lynn Bjorn was their boss. She would have to approve any moves they made.

"I called you first," Grappell admitted. "I'm in the process of writing up the request now but I know how important this case is to you. This guy is willing to talk and, if what he's saying is true, we can't waste time."

"Where does his family live?" Ree asked.

Grappell rattled off an address in North Dallas. Ree opened a kitchen drawer in search of a pen and paper before realizing she could just plug the address into her encrypted phone.

"Do you trust him?" Quint asked Grappell point-blank.

"Can we afford not to?" Ree asked, jumping in before Grappell could answer.

"Ree makes a good point," Grappell said. "How do I write this up?"

"This inmate is promising names with A-12, correct?" Quint asked.

"That's what he said," Grappell confirmed. "He seemed very nervous someone might already be on the way to get his wife and daughter."

Quint looked to Ree. "What do you think?"

She was already grabbing her purse and running shoes. "I think we have no choice but to get to them first."

"Call Bjorn and let her know what's going down," Quint stated as he followed Ree. "She won't want to read about this in a report. Especially if two innocent people end up dead—three, if they get to the inmate."

"Got it," Grappell confirmed. "I'll send over the inmate's name and information. He said his family might take some convincing, so you'll want to tell them some personal details about him. They'll ask about his birthday and his favorite book. You're supposed to give them his daughter's birthday and his favorite movie. The trick is that he doesn't like to read because he's dyslexic. That's how they'll know you were sent by him."

"You drive." Ree ushered Quint out the front door before locking it behind them. From the looks of it, they were headed to Dallas, and back in the thick of the case.

Chapter Two

Quint raced to his vehicle and slid into the driver's seat as Ree hopped into the passenger side. Cell phone in her palm, the target address filled her screen after a couple of taps. The urgency of the situation demanded they table any relationship conversation, which was probably for the best. No one had ever been able to hurt her the way Quint Casey could. She needed to remember that before she ended up with her heart ripped out of her chest.

At forty-two years old, the man had aged to perfection. He was tall and, basically, a solid wall of muscle. Don't even get her started on those sapphire-blue eyes of his, the storm brewing behind them making him even sexier. His muscled torso formed an improbable *V* at the waist and even with day-old stubble on his chin, the man would be considered hot by most standards. He had the kind of body most athletic recruiters would kill for if he was college age. He had the whole look—chiseled jawline, strong, hawklike nose and piercing eyes. Being intelligent put him in a whole new stratosphere.

Intense would be a good word to describe his personality, but he seemed like the type to intensely love someone if he ever truly let them inside. His upbringing had hardened him. He'd been born in a trailer park and raised by a single mother whom he unabashedly referred to as a saint. She'd worked two jobs after his father walked out not long after Quint was born, and she was the reason he got his act together when he'd gone astray in high school.

Now, he blamed himself for his former partner's death and the fact would probably haunt him for the rest of his life. Tessa Kind had been pregnant. She'd convinced him not to tell Bjorn right away, saying she needed time to adjust to the news. The child's father took off after she'd told him. Tessa had asked Quint to be the baby's godfather. The bust that took her life had been complicated by DEA involvement. Someone went left when they should have gone right. Tessa had been killed by mistake. One person had escaped the bust that night, Dumitru. Ree had read the file in detail after the Houston case.

A person like Quint wouldn't take letting down someone he loved lightly, and he'd loved Tessa more than if he'd had a blood-related little sister.

It was most likely the real reason he'd left the suitcase in his truck. He would never allow himself to be happy. He wouldn't see it as fair to Tessa. Since Ree couldn't compete with a ghost, she probably needed to protect her own heart. Quint Casey could wreck her.

The ride to Dallas was quiet as Quint concentrated

on the road, gripping the steering wheel like he was about to make damn sure it didn't go anywhere. *Brooding* would be a good word to describe the agent sitting next to her. He had his game face on, and a family was at stake.

"GPS says we're almost there," Ree said, breaking the silence.

Quint glanced at the clock. "Do you want to do the honors?"

"I'll shoot the text," Ree said, firing off the okay to Grappell to send in the federal agents, who'd been parked outside the prison gates in a white minivan for the last twenty minutes. "Axel Ivan will be in protective custody in the next five minutes."

Quint nodded but he didn't speak. He didn't have to for her to know what was running through his thoughts. Ivan might already be dead. He could be hanging in his prison cell by now. He'd taken a huge personal risk in speaking to Agent Grappell on the phone. One that could cost his life. And since the death rate for prisoners related to this case was high, Quint would be tense with worry until he knew Ivan was safely in custody.

Getting to the family before anyone else just took on a new priority now that they'd given the okay to extract Ivan. The North Dallas address was near, so Quint exited the Dallas North Tollway onto Frankford Road. He headed east toward Preston Road. Ivan's wife and daughter lived in a gated community to the right, past the grocery store and strip mall that was on the left.

Beyond the entrance was a large lake. The waterfall

was visible from the turn-in. Quint stopped at the guard shack and flashed his badge. The rent-a-cop was short and hefty. He didn't look like he could outrun a turtle. The weapon strapped to his side was most likely a commercial-grade stun gun. Not exactly stellar security but he would probably have 911 on speed dial, anyway.

"Go on through, sir." The security guard pressed a button—the gate almost immediately opened and he waved them in. Grappell would have already made arrangements for them to get past the first line of defense.

"Ivan's wife lives in a town house along the road that circles the community," she informed him. The houses in this area probably started at close to a million dollars. The place where his wife and kid lived would probably be about half to three quarters of the starter-home price in this neighborhood. Ree sighed. Unfortunately, crime paid.

It also came with a price and Ivan's family were targets now that the text came from Grappell, confirming the extraction.

"He's alive," Ree said to Quint. He grunted an acknowledgement. She didn't take offense. He was focused, concentrating all his energy on the task at hand, and probably fighting off the instinct to ask her to wait in the truck. He'd never treated her like anything but an equal.

Ree scanned the street. No one in this neighborhood parked out front. The road was quiet and clear. Too quiet? Too clear? Adrenaline kicked her body into high gear. Her senses sharpened as she went on full alert. A front-gate guard could be bought.

From the side-view mirror, Ree caught sight of a vehicle barreling toward them. Based on the map she'd studied on the way over, there were woods at the very back of the property. If leaving the way they came, which happened to be the lone entrance, was out of the question, they could get to the back wall, climb it and run into the woods. On the other side was a nice neighborhood that wasn't gated, and possible freedom.

If they'd had time, they could have planted an agent there. But the fewer people who knew about this extraction, the better.

"Do you see that?" she asked Quint but he was already studying the rearview mirror. He reached underneath the driver's seat and pulled out a Glock at the same time Ree gripped hers. Cell phone in one hand, she tried to snap a picture of the license plate of the black Acura gunning for them. The suspension had been tweaked, turning the vehicle into one of those lowriders with oversize tires.

"I'll swerve as he gets close, blocking the road. You bolt out the passenger side and get to Ivan's family," Quint said. Neither had to point out all this would be for nothing if they couldn't save Ivan's wife and daughter. He would clam up faster than a metal trap that had been stepped on by a bear.

"Let's do this," Ree said.

Quint stomped the brake, causing the truck to slant sideways before coming to a screeching halt. The second it slowed down, Ree wasted no time in making a run for it. The town house was half a block away and the Ivans lived in unit number three.

Thankfully, Ree had on tennis shoes and joggers. The August heat threatened to melt the bottom of her shoes before she reached the target. Summers in Texas weren't for the faint of heart. Gunfire caused her to duck and then run in a zigzag pattern to make herself a more difficult target. Cell phone in hand, she managed to fire off a text to Grappell. He would be on standby, waiting to hear from her. The only word she needed to send was help.

QUINT HAD POSITIONED the truck at an angle, blocking the small one-lane residential street as the souped-up Acura with blacked-out windows skidded to a stop fifteen feet away. Rubber tires scorched the pavement. The sun glared against the windshield, making it impossible to see who was driving or how many were inside the vehicle. He had no idea if the gunshot had come from the driver or a passenger. Either way, Quint lowered himself in the seat, making as small a target as humanly possible.

There was no way he could identify himself as an ATF agent if he wanted to stay under the radar. He glanced over to the passenger side of his truck and saw Ree disappear around the block.

The driver of the Acura revved the engine. A threat? Quint couldn't get a look at the driver or a decent shot.

He was responsible for every bullet fired and wouldn't risk a civilian getting hurt.

A front door swung open, and a woman stood at the threshold with a cell phone to her ear, looking more angry than scared and no doubt calling the cops. She must have thought the gunshot was a car backfiring. It would make sense with the Acura.

The Acura driver reversed the vehicle and then gunned it. The woman stepped onto her perfectly decorated porch and behind her impeccably designed landscaping. The houses, lawns and people were flawless in this million-dollar neighborhood.

Quint had to stop the driver before he got to Ree and the Ivans first. She had a decent head start but was on foot and would have to convince Axel's wife to trust her. Not exactly an easy accomplishment given Axel's criminal history. His wife would be trained to be suspicious of strangers, especially those trying to rush her from her home with her daughter to keep them safe. She would be reluctant to accept help from anyone without first receiving word from Axel.

Rather than chase the Acura, Quint backed up, then turned around to the direction he'd been going before jackknifing his vehicle. He would idle his truck in front of the town house and wait for the Acura to make a move. Either way, Quint could block access long enough to hopefully give Ree time to work her magic and get away.

The Acura came up behind Quint. The driver must have figured out Quint's plan. This way, he was at a slight disadvantage because he'd have to do everything in reverse. The driver was smart—Quint would give him that.

After putting the gearshift in reverse, he backed up before the Acura could get close enough to get a good shot off. The sound of a police siren split the air, but it was clear to Quint the squad car wouldn't arrive in time.

Quint grabbed a ball cap from the seat and threw it onto his head to shield as much of his face as possible from the Acura driver. He bolted out of the driver's seat, arms out in front of him with his Glock leading the way. Keeping low would allow him to use the truck to block any bullets as he came around the front of the vehicle. No matter what else happened, he couldn't allow the Acura driver to get to the town house before him.

A quick glance to his left as he rounded the front of the truck said Ree had either worked her way inside the town house, or gone around the back. Using the back door would be tricky considering the Ivans would most likely have some form of protection. An aggressive-sounding dog barked nearby. Close enough to belong to Mrs. Ivan? Other random dog barks had already been filling the air. Then, there was the siren. Close enough to let Quint know help was on the way. Far enough that people could be dead by the time it reached them.

He needed to stack the deck in his favor. For the moment, at least, the driver seemed hesitant to make a run for the town house on foot. Quint needed to make sure he stayed where he was.

The crack of a bullet echoed, and it pinged off the side of the truck. Quint ducked.

New game plan. He dropped down on all fours and took aim. His marksman training came in handy, as he fired a shot and hit the front left tire of the Acura. His second shot was dead on, as well, nailing the front right tire.

That should slow down the bastard when he tried to drive off.

The door of the Acura opened and closed. Suddenly, Quint was staring at a pair of black running shoes. The driver was either abandoning the vehicle or about to charge the town house. Either way, Quint couldn't let the guy off the hook and he sure as hell couldn't let him out of his sight.

At this point, Quint had no idea where Ree was or if she'd gotten the wife and kid to agree to run.

Not knowing was the worst feeling. His mind momentarily went back to when he'd paced up and down a hallway on the sterile white tile of Parkland Hospital's trauma unit, where Tessa had been airlifted to. Minutes had ticked by. Then, an hour was gone.

The news had been delivered by the ER doc and Bjorn. Quint snapped out of it before he hit the point of no return on that road again. The one that always led to a vicious cycle that kept him beating himself up.

The man from the Acura was making a run for it. Quint shook out of his funk and popped to his feet, bolting after the guy. The runner was much shorter than Quint and lighter. He was quick, with less bulk to carry, and the guy ran fast enough to make the college track team. Too bad he'd wasted his talents on being a criminal instead. An adrenaline push probably wasn't helping matters.

Since Speed Runner had abandoned his vehicle, Quint figured it was probably registered to a phantom person if it had a registration at all.

Speed Runner jumped a fence and Quint cursed. His lungs already burned as much as his thighs, but the jogging-suit-in-August-wearing bastard didn't get to win.

As Quint scaled the fence, Speed Runner turned and fired a wild shot. The bullet pinged the bricks on the corner of the home ten feet away because he hadn't taken the time to aim. In the next second, he was already scaling the ten-foot-high wooden privacy fence this area was famous for. No one wanted strangers to have the ability to see what went on in their backyard. No fences in the front, not even wire ones. North Texas backyards were sacred. Quint wished Speed Runner would have taken them on that tour instead. His chest wouldn't be burning nearly as badly right now. He was also fairly certain he'd be picking splinters out of his fingers long after this chase ended.

Five blocks over, Speed Runner started slowing. The first sign he was running out of steam at this blistering pace sent a wave of relief over Quint. He was a couple of steps behind the younger, faster runner but Quint had something this kid didn't—stamina.

The sirens were closing in on the neighborhood.

Could Quint get this guy and keep his own identity a secret? Security would have been alerted to allow them passage, but he wouldn't necessarily be told why. Quint would have to allow himself to be arrested, which would leave Ree on her own. She was fully capable of doing her job without him there to hold her hand.

And yet the thought of leaving his partner vulnerable ate at him from the inside out. Let this guy go and he could be a problem for Ree. He was still armed and dangerous. She was out here somewhere.

Speed Runner continued slowing down, and Quint maintained his pace. At this rate, he would catch up to Speed Runner in a matter of seconds. His lungs gasped for air but he knew exactly how far he could push his body, and he had a little more gas in the tank.

He was almost within reach, but Speed Runner whirled around and jabbed a knife into Quint's side. Quint was close enough to knock the weapon out of Speed Runner's hand as it went off. The bullet shot through a fence. Quint winced, praying there'd be no scream to indicate an innocent civilian had been hit.

Quint dove at Speed Runner's knees a second after he turned to run. He connected and heard an immediate snap. A broken bone would slow down this bastard. Stopping a second ago to shoot had cost the jerk his freedom. Speed Runner bounced to his good foot. From the corner of Quint's eye, he saw security running toward them. Speed Runner tried to shake him off, but his grip on Speed Runner's ankle was unbreakable. Quint rolled onto his back, grabbed Speed Runner's other ankle and squeezed. Speed Runner cried out in pain as Quint jerked the man's feet out from under him.

Speed Runner landed with a thud and a grunt as all air seemed to whoosh from his lungs. Before he could make another move, Quint rolled on top of him, flipped the guy facedown before he knew what hit him and then practically crushed him with powerful thighs as he secured him in place.

"Freeze," Security said.

"Detain this jerk until the police arrive while I check on my friend. His gun is over there," Quint motioned toward the metal glinting through blades of green grass a few feet away. "Do it now. I have to go."

Security complied, handcuffing Speed Runner before securing the weapon and calling it in. With no sign of Ree, Quint could only hope Speed Runner had acted alone.

Chapter Three

"Keep your head down and stay as quiet as you can for me. Okay?" Ree crouched in front of Axel's wife, Laurie, and his daughter, Ariana, as the two huddled together in between the brick home and Japanese boxwoods. The common shrubs had been elevated into a row of perfectly symmetrical round balls.

The sound of shots being fired nearby had caused her to duck into the shrubs. Could she circle back to the truck near the family home? Could she risk calling Quint? He could be hiding somewhere and even the slight buzz of his cell could give him away.

She couldn't risk it no matter how badly she wanted to reach out to him, to know he was safe. Their recent romantic relationship had nothing to do with how much her heart was hammering her ribs at the thought something had happened to him. He'd used himself as a distraction so she could get to Ivan's family.

Police sirens had abruptly stopped. Cops were on the scene. Since they were still undercover, no one could know about their ATF affiliation, so it was best for her to hide for now. Otherwise, she would be arrested along with Quint if he wasn't already in cuffs. They would have to go to jail, leaving Laurie and Ariana vulnerable to the next attack. And there would be another. News was already out about Axel turning witness based on the fact Speed Runner came after Axel's family. It was the only logical conclusion after Speed Runner showed up.

Laurie nudged Ree at the sight of two officers walking across the street, checking bushes. The hopeful look in her eyes said she had no idea. The so-called cops wore black uniforms, not navy blue. And they had on white sneakers, a dead giveaway that they didn't work for the DPD. Officers there wore black shoes. Their belts were all wrong, too. All they wore were badges and shoulder holsters. These men were imposters. Ree needed them to keep moving, as they continued to poke sticks into shrubs far away from the ones she and the Ivans were in.

How long could they stay hidden?

Ree gave a slight headshake to Laurie. Her brown eyes grew wide as she pulled her daughter a little closer. The teenager was a mini version of her mother, with a slightly longer nose, no doubt inherited from her father.

The Ivan women were beautiful, though. They could model for the Italian version of *Vogue*—both had brown eyes, long, slicked-back ponytails, and were tall with some curves along with olive-colored skin. They were the picture of perfection, all high cheekbones, small nose and soft lips. Their silky black hair framed their perfectly symmetrical faces. Laurie was dressed in a silky cream-colored pantsuit that hugged her figure to perfection while Ariana had on a jumper that fell to midthigh. Laurie's clothing could be described as sexy without crossing the line of being vulgar.

Axel was a beast of a man from the pictures Grappell had just texted to her, large frame, large head, and large nose. He seemed to hold those old-fashioned, gender-biased rules that meant a man was the sole provider and protector of his family. Ree couldn't relate to any of it, but to each his own. Some women wanted to be protected. Some women wanted to be handled like breakable china dolls. Some women wanted a credit card without a limit and all the free time in the world to look and be some wacked-out version of perfection.

Ree preferred the messy chaos of her own closet. She threw outfits together that sometimes worked and sometimes undeniably did not. Perfection was unattainable and, quite frankly, boring.

But that was just her opinion. She had to admit perfection looked pretty great on the Ivan women.

The fake cops moved from house to house, and it was only a matter of time before they would head this way. The street was quiet. If anyone was home, they seemed afraid to step on their front lawns. Rightfully so, since a police chopper was overhead. There'd been the screech of rubber burning, gunshots fired and police sirens in the last fifteen minutes. She didn't blame everyone for locking their doors and staying inside. In fact, she preferred it. There would be less chance of a civilian being in the wrong place at the wrong time and ending up with a bullet in their chest.

Come on, Quint. Why hadn't her partner called?

Ree held on to her phone, using the camera feature to zoom in and snap a few pictures. They would most likely be too grainy to get anything usable, but it never hurt to try. Her stomach clenched as she thought about any of those bullets ending up in her partner.

She checked her cell. There was no word from Quint or Grappell.

Laurie nudged Ree again. She looked up in time to see the "officers" cross the street, coming onto their side five houses down. It wouldn't be long before they were right on top of the trio.

Ree nodded and tried her level best to give a reassuring look to Laurie. Ariana's eyes were still squeezed shut, as she looked like she was blocking out the world. One look at the kid said she'd been overprotected to the nth degree, but this also demonstrated how much Axel Ivan loved his family. Ree couldn't stand her family's overprotective side, but she appreciated the amount of love and care he'd put in. The pair of them seemed to love him just as much. Laurie's first question once Ree had established her identity was whether or not her husband was all right. The concern that had etched lines in the near-perfect woman's forehead had been real. To her, Axel was like any other businessman who worked and took care of his family. It seemed easy for her to forget that he was on the wrong side of the law.

The second thing that had come out of Laurie's

mouth was that her husband was a good man and couldn't possibly have killed someone in prison. Her argument was that he'd gone to mass every week before prison. Strange argument for a criminal's wife to make on behalf of her husband. Apparently, moving weapons that killed others into the hands of very bad people who used said weapons to murder and maim didn't register as bad in Laurie's book. As long as her husband wasn't the one pulling the trigger, she seemed fine with his line of work.

This didn't seem like the time to educate his wife on the fact that Ivan would have had to kill for his boss if asked to, and probably already had. Ree decided to let the woman live in her fantasy world. It wasn't Ree's job to educate a criminal's wife. It was, however, her job to keep the woman and her daughter alive.

The fake cops were three houses down and time was running out. Ree had no qualms about outrunning the men in "uniform" herself. Laurie and Ariana didn't seem like the fast running types. She needed a diversion or a break. Since luck hadn't exactly been in her favor of late, she figured a distraction was her best shot.

Glancing around, she searched for something she could throw. She'd played enough softball in her youth to realize she could chuck a rock across the street. If she could get Dumb and Dumber over there to look in the opposite direction, maybe she could get Laurie and Ariana to run around the house to the backyard.

Then what?

"How well do you know your neighbors?" Ree asked.

"We keep to ourselves since Axel went to prison. We used to throw amazing parties..." She paused in dramatic fashion, like her life was somehow harder than most because she could no longer fire up the barbecue and have the neighborhood over for dinner now that her husband had been busted.

Sorry. Ree left her sympathy for criminals who deserved to go to jail at home.

Two houses. Ree could always point her gun at the men and hope like hell they listened to her when she made them handcuff each other. Oh, right. There were no handcuffs on their belts, either. Another dead giveaway.

She texted her exact location to Grappell and begged for a squad car to circle the street. Then held her breath and prayed he would get the message in time.

OUT OF BREATH, Quint pushed his legs to keep going despite the burn in his lungs. Ree had to be around here somewhere. She couldn't have gone too far without the truck. Could he text her without putting her at risk? She hadn't reached out to him. The annoying voice in the back of his mind picked that moment to remind him that she would if she was able to.

The thought wasn't exactly reassuring.

Quint figured Ree had two options—the trees in the back of the neighborhood, or get to Frankford Road, a busy six-lane street that led back to the tollway to the west and Preston, another busy street, to the east.

The path she chose would have depended largely on

the situation. There was no way to reason it out. She would follow the path of least resistance. Trees or road? At this point, it was a coin toss.

Of course, he could go back to his truck that, by now, would most likely be guarded by cops along with the Acura with the shot-out tires. A neighbor might be able to identify Quint in his ball cap. He took it off, and tucked it inside his back pocket. The guard shack might have a security uniform he could "borrow" for the time being.

Quint circled back toward the gate. A street over, he stopped in his tracks as he saw two cops smacking shrubs with a stick.

"Hey," one of the cops shouted, but something wasn't quite right about the guy. Even from halfway down the block, Quint could sense something was off. The uniform? The way the guy walked as he moved toward Quint? The cop didn't have the usual swagger. There was also another indicator. The belt was a little too light, and missing a few key tools.

Quint took off running, circling back to the way he came. He figured he could run a couple of blocks over, get these guys on the wrong track and then head back to the guard shack from a different angle.

As he turned the corner, he caught sight of something in the shrubs near one of the fake cops, a bright floral print of some kind. Could it be Ree and the Ivans?

Since only one of the "cops" was following him and the other was moving toward the shrubs in question, Quint needed a new plan. He spun around, pulled out his Glock and aimed at a mailbox on the opposite side of the street. He fired a round, figuring it would get their attention.

The move worked as planned, so he booked it out of there. With both supposed officers on his tail, he needed to hop the wall blocking the neighborhood off from Frankford Road so he could get the lay of the land. His cell buzzed inside his pocket and relief washed over him.

Continuing in a dead run, he fished the phone out of his pocket and checked the screen. It was her. He answered and tried to speak through labored breaths.

"Thank you," she whispered, and he could hear the rustle of shrubbery.

"I'll bring these guys out to the front of the neighborhood. Can you get to the trees?" he asked.

"No can do," she said. "Cops are already there."

"Then I'll get these guys over the wall and to the strip mall across the street. I'll lose them in the grocery parking lot," he offered.

"I'm already requesting a car to meet us at the gate," she stated, sounding winded.

"If I'm not there in ten minutes, leave without me," he instructed.

"Got it," she said before ending the call. Neither could afford to take their attention off the goal. Hers was to get the Ivans to the guard shack safely. His was to lose the jerks following him and join up with Ree. Easy peasy.

Quint knew he was in trouble when he started whipping out corny lines. He'd been ignoring the red dot on his shirt that was flowering like lilies on a sunny morning after a spring rain. There was no way he was seriously hurt. The bullets had flown near him, some getting a little too close for comfort, but he would have registered a hit.

Exhaustion was setting in because he'd been running, then in a fight, and now back to running without much in his stomach in the way of food. Or caffeine. He never got a chance to finish his cup of coffee at Ree's, he thought as he leaped over a bush. He misjudged the height, caught his toe on a vine and went down face-first.

Branches stabbed his arms, torso and neck as he tried to tuck and roll out of the shrubbery. Whoever planted that thing deserved to be shot. But he couldn't allow himself to wallow in self-pity because the fake cops had rounded the corner and their smirks told him everything he needed to know about what they planned to do to him if they caught up.

Pain be damned, Quint untangled his shirt from the grip of the shrub and pushed up to his feet. There wasn't anything to grab hold of as he got hit with a bout of light-headedness.

He tried to take a step forward, but did a face-plant instead, eating grass and dirt. This was not good. This wasn't part of the plan. This wasn't supposed to be happening to Quint Casey, one of the ATF's finest agents.

The sounds of heavy footsteps and panting breaths drew closer as Quint tried to force open his eyes. Darkness tugged at the back of his mind, but he refused to give in. *Shake it off, Casey.*

Why couldn't he?

Chapter Four

Quint had distracted the fake cops. Ree stayed put as the text from Grappell said Dallas PD was coming. An SUV rounded the corner as she stepped out from the bushes. She waved her arms in the air, uncertain where Quint had gone. This scenario had gone south and Grappell had been forced to divulge information about her and the Ivans. As of now, Grappell was working on a safe house.

The officer stopped the vehicle. Over the loudspeaker, he asked for the three of them to come out of the bushes with their hands up. Ree's were already held up high.

"Do as the officer says," Ree urged Laurie and Ariana. The teen clung to her mother as though her life depended on it. They complied as the officer exited his vehicle.

"I understand the three of you are in need of a ride," he stated as they walked toward him.

"That's correct, sir," Ree said. "However, there are four of us."

"I was told three." The officer shook his head.

"I'd like to verify the information once we're en route," Ree stated. Bjorn must want Quint arrested if she didn't make provisions for him yet. He might be able to get information while in jail.

"I'm Officer Reinhart. I need to pat you down." The tall officer with a runner's build wore Ray-Ban sunglasses. "My SO said I need to put on a show for the neighbors."

Ree gave a slight nod.

"Hands on the vehicle," Officer Reinhart demanded.

She gave a slight nod to the Ivans before walking to the front of the vehicle and placing her palms on the hood. Laurie and Ariana followed suit, daughter sticking close to her mother.

The officer gave a quick pat-down, nothing to cause concern of abuse of power. Ree climbed in the back of the vehicle along with the others. She slipped her cell phone out of her pocket, careful to hide the fact she was texting to any watchful eyes. She bent forward, resting her elbows on her knees as the officer took his seat. A tow truck passed by on the road behind them. It was the same direction Quint had taken off to.

She texted Grappell that the three of them were safe inside the back of the SUV. And then she asked about Quint.

When Grappell commented on her and the Ivans but not on Quint, her heart sank. It meant there was no word from him. This seemed like a good time to remind herself he was a professional who was the best at his job.

He'd most likely been in stickier situations than this and would come out the other side just fine.

Pinching her nose, Ree leaned back in the seat as the officer finished typing on the laptop that was affixed to his vehicle. He drove off as she kept an eye out for her partner.

"Where are we going?" Laurie asked in barely a whisper.

"To a safe place," Ree commented. She couldn't tell Laurie what she didn't know—an exact location. She could only pray Quint had been picked up and was on his way to the safe house, the same as them.

The officer pulled onto the North Dallas Tollway, NDT, and headed south. Ree read the signs as they passed. First Campbell. Next, Arapaho, followed by Beltline. Then Spring Valley to Alpha. Reinhart took the Alpha Road exit then made his way to Midway Road and headed north again toward the Addison Airport, where he navigated his way into the parking lot of Million Air Dallas.

"This is the end of the line for me," Reinhart said, nodding toward a waiting Suburban with blacked-out windows.

"Thank you," Ree said, then added, "but you'll have to open the door for us if you're ready for us to exit the vehicle."

The officer exited the driver's seat and then opened the door. "If you ladies need further assistance, I'm sure your boss will let mine know."

"My name is Henry and I'll be driving you today.

Agent Grappell said to make you comfortable," the driver said through a rolled-down partition. All she could see was a traditional blue chauffeur's hat along with mirror-lensed glasses. "There's cold water in the cooler, sealed bottles."

"Thank you. We're good," Ree said before the partition came up and they were effectively sealed off from the outside world. The Ivans made themselves at home immediately, relaxing in the leather seats. Laurie pulled two bottles of sparkling water from the small cooler, handing one over to her daughter as she exhaled.

These two looked like they belonged riding around in a vehicle like this with a driver at the ready and refreshments at arm's reach. Ree couldn't decide if she was sad for them. Everything in their world seemed manicured and catered A strange ache filled Ree. She'd come to resent Sunday suppers at her mother's ranch due to her mother's disapproval of Ree's career, but they'd been good once. Thinking back, it was a tradition her father had started since long before she could remember before he died when she was eleven years old.

Ree pulled out her cell and palmed it, praying for a message from Grappell about Quint. She started to request an update but realized she would probably be the first person he contacted the second he received word.

Rather than try to sit back in her seat, which she realized was impossible under the circumstances, she leaned forward and checked her inbox. Scrolling through names that barely registered, her thoughts kept drifting back to Quint. If he was safe, he would have made contact by now. The fact he hadn't checked in with Grappell after luring away the fake cops distressed her.

Was he still in the neighborhood? She'd watched for him on Frankford Road, past the apartments to the right and the shopping center with the Albertsons grocery store and her Tex-Mex favorite at the end of the mall. There'd been no sign of him on the brick wall encasing the neighborhood to the left. She'd kept an eye there as well.

The fake cops had to have caught up with him. It was the only explanation that made sense. He couldn't outrun them and now he was…

Ree stopped herself right there. It was possible Quint had escaped and his cell phone had gotten lost in the process. Again, she reminded herself how fully capable he was of taking care of himself. She also decided to point out her concern wasn't more than caring for her partner. They'd been through some rough times on the cases they'd worked together so far and they'd bonded. Caring about what happened to each other was part of what made them good partners.

The partition rolled down.

"This is where I'm supposed to drop you off," the driver said. A text came through as he added, "You should be receiving a message any second with an address."

She thanked the driver and ushered Laurie and Ariana out of the vehicle. Neither looked too thrilled to be exiting the safety of the Suburban.

An address came through via a text from Grappell. Ree brought up her map feature as the Suburban pulled away—2436 Briarwood Lane. They'd been dropped off at the Farmer's Branch Moose Lodge across the street from the neighborhood. They would walk Towerwood Drive across Webb Chapel Road, which would lead them into the neighborhood of the safe house on Briarwood Lane.

"How much farther do we have to go?" Laurie asked, holding tight to her daughter, who looked ready to burst into tears. They were sweaty and breathing hard.

"Almost there," Ree reassured her, thinking gratitude might be a better tact to take instead of whining. Then again, she would never understand anyone who chose the kind of life they lived over the straight and narrow. Ree's life might not be champagne and Italian leather shoes, but she had a lot of pride in knowing she'd worked for everything she owned. Her car. Her home. Her furnishings.

The safe house looked like any other home on the block, a one-story tan-and-brown brick. The wooden door had a peephole. Ree stood in front of it so she could clearly be seen. She texted Grappell the second they were standing on the small concrete block porch. The grass in this area was a patchy yellow-green. There were more weeds than lawn. The trim on the house was in severe need of a paint job, but it fit in with the neighbors. This safe house had a pair of ATF agents acting as spouses while on another case.

The door swung open, and an agent ushered them inside.

"I live here with my 'wife' and have a lot of cousins come visit," the agent said by way of explanation of their cover. He was a solid six feet tall with curly brown hair that looked to be in need of a cut. He had on a Gap T-shirt and cotton shorts with flip-flops to round out the look. Ree guessed him to be close in age to her, in his mid-thirties.

"Is there a place where my daughter and I can wash up?" Laurie asked.

"Yeah, sure," he said, then pointed to a small hallway right off the living room.

Laurie thanked him and scurried off as Ree shot him a look.

"They can't go anywhere. Bars on the windows," he reassured her. "My name is Lucas Hoover."

"Like the vacuum?" Ree asked.

"Like the president," Lucas stated with a hint of pride and a smirk.

"I'm Ree, but you probably already know that," she said after a firm handshake. He wouldn't know much else except who she was and that she was bringing friends. She checked her cell in case there was a message from Grappell.

"No word on your partner yet?" Lucas asked.

She shook her head.

"What can I set you up with?" he asked. "A quick tour?"

"Sounds good," she stated, thinking the living room

was a relic from the nineties. Gold wallpaper with a print design. The seating was decent—a sofa and a couple of leather club chairs and benches positioned in a circle for talking. The room immediately opened up to a dining area with sliding glass doors behind the table. To the left was a standard kitchen with all-white appliances and hunter green wallpaper. The table seated six and had laptops set up at two of the spots. She imagined those were for him and his "wife."

He walked her down the same hallway Laurie and Ariana had disappeared to a few minutes ago. The sink water was running as they passed the bathroom. There were two bedrooms on the left and at the end of the hall to the right was the master. It had its own bathroom, which Ree assured Lucas she didn't need to see.

"Are you hungry?" he asked as they made their way back into the kitchen area.

"Not me," she said, checking her cell for messages again. "I'll ask A and B," she said, referring to the women they were assigned to protect.

"There's food in the fridge. Drinks, too. Make yourselves at home. My wife's name is Chelsea Ridder. She 'works' a regular job and our cover is that I work from home. We both work in tech. She's a graphic designer and I'm a programmer."

"Sounds good," Ree said. She was listening despite the fact she checked her phone two more times. And then it buzzed in her hand. Her heart pounded inside her rib cage as her pulse skyrocketed.

Quint has been shot at, stabbed, and arrested.

Ree glanced up at Lucas. "My partner has been stabbed."

"Where is he?" Lucas immediately reached inside his pocket for what she assumed was keys.

"Jail," she said as a half-dozen scenarios raced through her mind, none of them good.

THE LAST THING Quint remembered was hearing sirens, then heavy footsteps. As he'd blacked out, the perps bolted in the opposite direction. He woke in a jail cell. No phone. No gun. No wallet. Since he didn't keep his badge inside his black fold-over wallet, anyway, he had no way to ID himself as law enforcement. Plus, he was still undercover.

His shirt was soaked in blood. His? He'd been bandaged up.

Quint tried to sit up. Pain shot through him as the memories came back of being chased, the fight and being stabbed by Speed Runner. At least Speed Runner was locked behind bars somewhere inside this place.

As Quint tried to move, he felt the effects of being in a knife fight. Still, his thoughts flew to Ree. He'd drawn the fake cops away from her. Did she get away? Was she safe? His chest squeezed at the thought anything could have happened to her. The Ivans were the least of his worries. The lead drying up wouldn't matter if he lost Ree. Catching Dumitru would have no meaning if there wasn't something to look forward to when the case was closed.

A uniformed officer came into the room with a set of keys in hand. His tan shirt and matching pants with brown stripes down the sides of his legs signaled he was a jailer. He had salt-and-pepper hair, wrinkles that said he was closing in on retirement age and a thick enough accent Quint that figured the guy said *y'all* a fair amount.

"You're out, Matthews," the officer said. His name tag read Rex Davis. Given his height and lankiness, he probably grew up with a nickname like T-Rex.

"How is that?" Quint asked, playing the part. He'd been arrested dozens of times for the sake of a case in the past. It was nothing new. The charges against him included disorderly conduct and disturbing the peace. An investigation was pending that might add charges.

"You made bail. Sally Struthers posted for you. Said she was your mother," Rex continued.

Sally Struthers? Quint shook his head. Grappell should definitely get a gold star for that one. He always referenced stars from old TV shows his dad used to watch. Once Quint got his cell phone back, he'd text his response—*All in the Family.*

Speaking of which, he asked, "Any chance you have my cell inside there?" He motioned toward the paper bag in T-Rex's hand.

"Just a black wallet," the officer said.

No keys? Then Quint remembered he'd left them in

the vehicle near the Ivan house. "Is my mother outside waiting?"

The officer walked Quint to the front, closing and locking doors behind them. A few minutes later, they stood in the lobby, where Quint was handed the paper bag. "Said she'd be in the blue Honda."

Quint's heart stirred at the thought of seeing Ree again.

Chapter Five

“Thank you, sir,” Quint said, figuring he needed to leave on a positive note. His thoughts raced and he wouldn’t get information until he got inside the Honda.

Outside, a blue Civic waited. An agent sat in the driver’s seat, motioning for him to hurry. He did, covering his disappointment it wasn’t Ree in the driver’s seat. In fact, he couldn’t get away from the jail fast enough.

The sun was setting, which at this time of year, meant it was after 8:00 p.m. He’d been out cold for hours. He hopped into the passenger seat. His body screamed in pain with the slightest movement. Fresh blood soaked a bandage as he checked underneath his shirt.

He didn’t exchange names with the other agent. There was no need.

“I have a partner,” Quint said once the door was closed and he was able to strap in his seat belt. “We got separated.”

“All I know is that she’s fine and at the safe house, where I’m dropping you off,” the agent said. “Sally” was really a man in a wig. Once they pulled out of the parking lot and stopped at the first red light, he took off the wig and tossed it in the back seat. The wig meant he'd been pulled from an undercover assignment to help out.

"Thanks for picking me up," Quint stated. Granted, it was the guy's job but Quint always appreciated a fellow agent's time. Being undercover was difficult enough without being tagged to pick up someone from jail and risk blowing their cover.

"Not a problem," the agent said.

Quint didn't spend a whole lot of time memorizing the details of the guy's face. He stopped at the bright red lipstick and overdone rouge. The rest of the drive was spent in silence. Quint leaned his seat about as far back as it could go.

Before long, the agent stopped the Honda in front of a one-story brick house in a suburban neighborhood.

"Sorry if I bled on your seat," Quint said.

"Don't worry about it," the agent said. "It'll only help with my credibility."

Quint cracked a smile that felt like it broke his ribs in half.

"Mind if I ask a personal question, though?" the agent asked.

"Go ahead." Answering was the least Quint could do.

"Are you, by any chance, *the* Quint Casey?" the agent asked.

"Guilty as charged" was all Quint said as he opened the door. Getting in and out of the sedan was painful.

"Interesting," the agent stated. "It's been a pleasure working with someone like you even for a quick pickup."

"I appreciate the compliment," Quint said and meant it.

"You're a legend in the agency," the agent said.

All Quint could do was smile at that one.

"Believe about half of what you hear about me," Quint joked.

The agent laughed. "Will do, sir."

Quint closed the door and headed to the house. As he stepped onto the concrete block porch, the door swung open and Ree came bolting toward him. He was so damn happy to see her that he forgot to warn her not to touch him too hard. When she barreled into his chest and wrapped her arms around him, he let out a grunt.

Ree pulled back and apologized.

"Don't be sorry," he said. "You're the best thing that's happened to me today."

She looked him up one side and down the other. "This blood is fresh. You're turning ghost-white. Let's get you inside."

Ree moved beside him and wrapped an arm around him for support. He leaned on her, needing the extra help to get inside.

Quint stumbled. He was dizzy and saw stars as he was led to a bedroom, where he was helped onto the bed. "I should clean up first before I bleed all over the place."

Those were the last words he remembered saying.

The next time Quint opened his eyes, there was a

worried-looking doctor hovering over him. Then, later, he awoke to a dim light on the nightstand and Ree asleep in a chair next to the bed between him and the door.

By the first light of morning, Quint felt awake enough to sit up. The second he moved, Ree bolted up.

"How do you feel?" she asked. The concern in her voice told him it had been a rough night.

"Better," he said. "I have one helluva headache, though. Any chance there's coffee brewing?"

"I heard one of the agents named Lucas up half an hour ago. I can check." She pushed up to standing and started toward the door.

Quint figured he could make it across the hall to the bathroom on his own. Standing made him feel woozy. The room started to spin, so he took a step toward the dresser and held on for the ride. He'd had worse benders than this, he tried to convince himself. Except he wasn't much of a drinker. A beer here and there was as far as it had gone. He'd grown up around too much alcoholism in the trailer park to ever fall down that hole.

His stomach gurgled and growled. He probably should have asked for a power bar before trying to put any caffeine in his stomach. At this point, he'd take either.

Making it across the hall took some effort. He was certain "Sally" from the Honda wouldn't be too impressed with his skills at this moment. Quint made himself laugh, and that just hurt.

He washed his face and located a toothbrush still in its wrapper. Safe houses kept various supplies on hand for when they were needed. There would be clothing in various sizes. After brushing his teeth, he felt half-human again. The walk back to the bedroom went a bit easier. He shrugged out of his shirt, and the simple act was more painful than he ever imagined.

It slid out of his hand and onto the floor. Quint looked down at the crumpled shirt. Too bad. There was no way he would be able to pick it up. A clean one waited in the dresser. He located his size and tossed it onto the bed for later.

Ree appeared at the doorway, carrying a tray. She stopped the second her eyes dropped to his bare chest. Suddenly, her cheeks flushed. She cleared her throat. She'd seen him completely naked before, so her reaction caught him off guard. Was it the circumstances or did she regret going there with him on their last assignment?

The suitcase. Could this tie back to the fact he'd shown up at her doorstep without it in his hand? Did she want to dial back the relationship?

"I brought food," she said. "And coffee."

Without making eye contact, she moved to the bed and set down the tray.

"Do you need help sitting down again?" she asked, her gaze steady on the bandages on his chest.

"I got it." At least, he hoped he had it. "Mind if I take your chair instead?"

"No. Go right ahead." She scooted the tray closer as he grabbed both arms of the chair, steadily lowering himself down. "What hurts?"

"Everything," he said, wincing as he reached for the fork. The scrambled eggs and bacon looked and smelled amazing.

"Lucas made this for you. Chelsea, the one who drove you here, had to leave so she said she'd check in later," Ree stated.

He didn't like how easily Lucas's name rolled off her tongue.

"Have you been getting to know each other?" he asked, realizing how jealous that sounded.

"Us three, you mean?" she quipped, cocking an eyebrow. "Not to mention Laurie and Ariana Ivan."

Point taken.

"GRAPPELL SENT A message an hour ago stating we can watch the interview with Axel Ivan since we were rerouted to save his family earlier," Ree said, steering the conversation to work. There was no way she was letting him get away with the jealous routine now. He'd been clear on where he stood with her when he'd left the suitcase in the car. Fizzle.

"Good. Did he say when we should leave?" Quint asked, wincing as he leaned forward to grab the tray and position it in his lap.

"You're hurt," she reminded him. "There's no reason to start making plans to ditch out of here in your condition. Plus, you haven't met Laurie and Ariana yet."

"Where are they?" he asked.

"In the bedroom. I'm giving them a minute to adjust

and process everything that has happened and changed in their lives," she stated.

"Good idea. As for me, I've felt worse, looked worse," he said before taking a bite of egg and chewing. He followed it with a sip of coffee and some of the tension lines in his face eased.

"Not on my watch, you haven't," she stated. "You'd be a liability if we left here and something happened."

Quint looked poised to argue, then took another bite instead.

"Your health has to come first and the doctor said you need to take it easy," she stated.

"Can't," he said without missing a beat.

"Or won't?" she asked.

"Does it matter?" He sounded annoyed.

"It does to me," she countered. His anger was him covering the fact he was weak right now. It was also his frustration coming out. Despite those things being true, she couldn't let him run around half-cocked and in terrible physical condition. In fact, she needed to tell him what she'd been thinking since finding out he'd been stabbed. "You know, you could stay here until WITSEC arrives. Hand off Laurie and Ariana, then heal. You have to give your body the time it needs, or you could end up in real trouble, Quint."

"Did you have a replacement in mind?" He picked up the toast and ripped off a piece before tossing it in his mouth.

"I mean, the obvious choice is here on property," she

continued, and she could almost see his temperature rising by the redness in his cheeks.

"Tell Lucas that he can—"

"It's not Lucas I was suggesting," she said, cutting him off. "It was Chelsea. Why would your mind automatically snap to him?"

"Guess I was wrong." Quint didn't say another word while he finished every last bite of food and then drained his coffee mug. "We both know this is my case, Ree."

"Plans can change," she stated. Having grown up with four brothers, she knew a thing or two about being stubborn. Quint was digging in his heels due to his personal involvement in the case. "And we both know this is how cases go sideways."

"If you don't think I'm competent, that's fine," he said. "But this is my case and I can easily request to be the one to work with Chelsea instead of you."

"What do you think Bjorn's response is going to be?" she asked. There'd been a whole lot of desperation in his voice.

Quint picked up the tray from his lap and bent forward to set it on the bed.

"For what it's worth, I was worried sick about you," she finally said on a sharp sigh. "I have no doubts about your abilities as an agent, Quint. But you have to admit, sometimes it's better for someone to stay back and call in plays from the desk. Or, in your case, bed."

"We can work my injuries into the cover story," he said. "We used the fake boot before and it worked."

"Because it was a fake injury," she reminded him. "This is very real. You were stabbed and I had no idea where you were or what kind of condition you were in."

Quint managed to join her at the foot of the bed. He pulled her against his chest, where she heard the staccato rhythm of his heartbeat.

"I don't know what I would have done if anything had happened to you," she admitted, leaning into him.

He brushed a kiss on her lips before resting his forehead against hers.

"I'm right here," he reassured her. "I'm a little damaged but I'm okay."

He was alive and there was a difference.

A hot tear rolled down her cheek. It was all she could afford since she didn't want to give away the fact that she and Quint had crossed a line in their professional relationship. The sound of footsteps coming toward them from down the hallway caused her to sit upright and start checking his bandages.

She cleared her throat as she heard Lucas at the door. "The doctor said these have to be redressed every night. You have to wrap yourself in Saran Wrap to take a shower so they'll stay dry."

Lucas stepped inside the room and introduced himself. He and Quint shook hands and then he thanked him for the meal.

"There's more coffee if you're ready for another cup," Lucas said. His gaze bounced from Quint to Ree and back. He was on to them. Based on his expression, he'd picked up on the attraction simmering between them.

"I'll be right there," Quint said and his voice was husky, basically a dead giveaway.

This wasn't good. News like this could get around and damage both of their reputations. Ree bit back a curse. They weren't used to working so closely with other agents, people who would pick up on their underlying chemistry.

"Right," Lucas said. "Good to see you sitting up again."

Ree stood. "I'll refill your coffee."

"Okay, thanks," Quint said in what must be one of the most awkward conversations Ree had ever been engaged in with coworkers.

She grabbed his mug and made a beeline for the kitchen. She'd go pretty much anywhere to get out of that room at this point, so she could regroup and figure out how to spin what Lucas had just seen happening between her and Quint.

Chapter Six

“I’d like to get up and walk,” Quint said. “How about we join Ree in the kitchen?”

“Sounds good to me,” Lucas agreed.

Quint managed the trip to the next room without letting his face give away the sheer amount of pain he was in. He immediately locked gazes with Ree as he headed to the table and sat down.

“Your phone has gone MIA. Service was shut off and data was erased remotely,” Lucas informed as Quint motioned for the agent to take a seat. Lucas obliged. “It’s great to have an opportunity to work with someone of your caliber.”

Quint never knew what to say to a comment like Lucas’s, so he went with “Thanks.”

“I’ve heard about some of your busts,” Lucas continued. He smiled like he was about to start recounting them and then his expression became solemn. “Tessa Kind was an amazing agent.”

“Yes, she was,” Quint confirmed.

“I was sorry to hear,” Lucas continued.

The subject was still sore with Quint even though he appreciated how many lives Tessa had touched. Others seemed genuinely sorry about the loss. It warmed Quint's heart to think her memory was still alive in the agency.

"I appreciate the sentiment," Quint said. In a surprise move, even to himself, he added, "I miss her."

"How could you not?" Lucas stated. "She was intelligent and knew her stuff. Her sense of humor was legendary. She kept me on the straight and narrow early on in my career. She was a damn fine agent."

"Did you know Tessa personally?" Quint asked, caught off guard at all the compliments.

"I worked with her on my first undercover case," Lucas admitted.

Quint rocked his head. Tessa had the patience to work with newbies, whereas he'd rather stick tacks in his eyelids. Patience in a case was one thing. Patience in working with new people wasn't something Quint had ever been able to tolerate despite Bjorn's pleas for him to make an exception every once in a while. It just wasn't in his DNA.

"She kicked my butt more than once," Lucas said, his gaze unfocused, like he was looking inside himself for details of the memory. "We were working a tobacco case. Truckloads were being moved across the border and sold illegally out of the back of a store with no license. The owner had a record and couldn't qualify for a liquor license. We took the guy down but I probably made every stupid mistake in the book."

Quint closed his eyes, thinking all the quips Tessa would have had about a case like that one.

"Tessa not only walked me through how to bust the guy, but she tripped him when I lost my grip and he started to get away. She made eyes at me because I was standing there dumbfounded at how this guy could have slipped right out of my hands. She gave me a look that said I better get my act together and bust this guy," Lucas continued. "Training kicked in and I've never hesitated on a bust since. The thing is, she never teased me about it or told anyone."

Quint knew how that would have gone over with a few agents—not so well. They would have given Lucas a nickname based on something they witnessed during the bust that would have stuck with the young man the rest of his career. Law enforcement was like a fraternity and the hazing could get intense with some officers.

"She would never do that if she believed in you," Quint said. "If she didn't, she would have taken it to Bjorn in private after telling you she thought you might want to consider another profession."

"So I've heard," Lucas said. "She gave me the confidence to keep going when I faltered, and I've never forgotten it." Lucas looked down at the carpet. "I would have liked to say something at her funeral but there was a line of agents in front of me."

There was a time in the not-so-distant past that hearing Tessa's name used to make Quint sad. Now, it didn't. It only served to remind him what a good person she was and oddly made him feel closer to her memory.

"Tessa had this crazy laugh once you got her going," Quint said.

"Like an elephant, right?" Lucas chuckled.

"Exactly, and then she'd snort when she really got going," Quint stated as Ree joined them with two mugs in her hand. He took one from her as she took a seat.

"She once spewed tea on the windshield of my service vehicle," Lucas said.

"And then probably blamed you for it since you were the one who made her laugh," Quint said.

"As a matter of fact, she did." Lucas laughed. "She threatened to make me clean it up if I ever made her laugh that hard again."

There was something special about having Ree in the room while Quint and Lucas relived the memories of Tessa. Ree had a calming presence that took away some of the ache in his chest.

"I usually got socked in the arm," Quint revealed. "And she could pack a punch."

"For a tiny person, she had the strength of a bear," Lucas added.

The two shared a few more stories, then Ree's cell buzzed. She checked the screen. "A message from Agent Grappell."

Quint took a sip of coffee, pretending not to be hanging on by a thread to learn there's been a breakthrough in the case.

"He says a marshal will be by in an hour to pick up Laurie and Ariana. Once they're safe, Axel will be ready to talk," she stated as she read the text.

"We'll be ready." Lucas pushed up to standing. "I better get some food in them. I'll go ask what they're hungry for. No telling how long they'll be on the road when they're relocated."

Quint nodded, appreciating a few minutes alone with Ree.

The minute Lucas was out of earshot, Ree said, "That can't happen again. He almost caught us in a very intimate moment."

"I know," he said.

"It's unprofessional and word will get around, ruining both of our reputations," she continued, as if he hadn't just agreed.

"You don't have to talk me in to anything," he said. "I'm on your side on this."

"Good." She pressed her lips together like she was biting back what she really wanted to say. "Because I can't have a mark on my file or every single male agent I work with from here on out wondering if he has a chance with me if we work a case together because Lucas walked into that bedroom at the wrong moment."

"Agreed," he said. The thought of Ree being hit on by another agent sent anger boiling in his veins. The suitcase incident was the equivalent of one step forward, two steps back, in their relationship.

"You can't afford female agents to wonder if they should make a move or wait for you to, either," she said emphatically. "It'll hurt both of us for promotions if Bjorn got word."

"Maybe we shouldn't spend a whole lot of time worrying about it," Quint said, figuring he had to stop her momentum before she talked them into a harassment case.

"You are a decent-looking guy," she continued. "Women are going to want to date you. Look at you." She threw her hands up in the air.

"If it matters at all, I don't want to date other women. I'd like to date you but I realize how complicated I am, so that's not as easy as it probably should be," he finally said. "Let's move on and not worry about looking back right now."

Those words were meant to be reassuring. Instead, Ree reacted like she'd been punched in the gut.

RATHER THAN LET the comment get to her, Ree lifted her chin and took a measured sip of coffee. A couple of slow, deep breaths later and she could think more clearly. "Tell me how you really feel."

He started to open his mouth but she stopped him with a raised hand.

"I mean physically," she said with a cautionary tone. They'd reached a standstill instead of moving forward with their personal relationship. It happened. It was called hitting a wall. Neither had the equipment to tunnel through. "Be real with me, Quint."

"The stabbing hurts. I still bleed a little when I move but I imagine that will scab up after another night of sleep. I'm banged up pretty good but I've pushed through in worse shape, so I know I'll be able to handle whatever comes my way," he stated. "I'll have to be quicker with a gun and back off from a fist fight. I'd say by tomorrow, I'll be in decent enough shape to sit in on the Axel Ivan interview."

Ree listened, taking in the information. Bottom line, she could request to have Quint removed from the case, but she couldn't do that to him yet. He needed a chance to prove himself capable and she needed to help him see this thing through. She'd made a promise she had no intention of going back on now. Besides, with two undercover operations under her belt and a need to find justice for a fellow agent, Quint wasn't the only one personally invested. Plus, she wanted to be the one to help Quint move on with his life after Tessa. She wanted to help give him the closure he needed to pick up the pieces of his life again.

"Okay," she said. "I'm all in with you, Quint."

The look he gave said she'd caught him off guard.

"What? Did you think I was going to walk away and leave you hanging?" she said, faking being offended in dramatic fashion. The mood needed to be lightened if they were going to continue to work together.

Quint laughed, then winced.

"Don't strain yourself," she teased, lifting up her coffee cup.

"I can probably still do legwork," he said. "If I don't move something, I'll lose my mind sitting around all day."

"We should head into the living room. Start with walking and see how the bleeding goes?" she offered.

"That's probably a good idea." His lips curled into a smirk.

"I know. Patience has never been your forte unless it directly relates to a case," she quipped.

"I can't deny that," he stated, setting down his mug on the table before slowly standing.

"You start bleeding and we dial it back," she warned.

"Yes, ma'am," he said with that same heart-melting smirk. There was something incredibly sexy about the way Quint smiled.

"Why don't you lean some of your weight on me until the room stops spinning," she instructed.

"How do you know the room is spinning?" He put an arm around her shoulder.

"I can see it in your eyes, Casey." She gave him "the look." Part of her wanted to argue for him to go back to bed and heal. The part that grew up with four brothers said the more she pushed a stubborn person like Quint, the more he would push back. He needed to walk around and test out his body a little bit to see where he stood. He wouldn't be able to figure that out lying in a bed. And he didn't have to tell her any of that for her to know what he was doing sitting in the kitchen instead.

"What was that look for?" he asked.

"You seem to forget I grew up with a bunch of brothers and a grandfather," she stated, regretting the statement as soon as it left her mouth. She sounded like a jerk reminding him of the lonely childhood he'd had in comparison, being the only child of a single mother who worked long hours to make ends meet.

Quint took a couple of steps and then leaned heavily on her. She wrapped her arm around his midsection to keep him from falling over and managed to touch a sore spot. He winced and grunted.

"Sorry," she said.

"Don't be," he countered, grabbing on to the doorjamb. "I have to push through this and get a true gauge of what I can do."

"A day makes a big difference when it comes to healing injuries, in my experience," she said.

"When have you been hurt?" he asked.

"Growing up with four brothers?" she quipped. "Every couple of days it seems like. I've fractured two fingers, my left wrist and my clavicle." She flashed eyes at him. "Don't ask."

"Scout's honor," he said, the spark in his eyes returning for the first time since she'd seen him in this condition.

"We both know you were never a Scout," she teased.

"You're not wrong there." He smiled as he took another step.

"Then there was the summer I spent in a cast because I broke my arm right when I fell off the tire swing," she continued, distracting him with her story so he would hopefully not focus on how much pain he was in. "Witnesses agree that I was pushed, but Finn argues it to this day."

"Out of curiosity, what did Finn think he was doing?" Quint made it to the hallway.

"He swears he was pushing the swing to make it go

faster and his hands slipped," she said. "We all know he wanted me off the swing."

"Somehow, I'm sure you didn't let him get away with that," Quint said with a laugh that made every muscle in his torso tense up.

"No, but then my mom got mad at me because she said I hit him out of spite," she said, thinking her rocky relationship with her mother went as far back as she could remember.

"Was she right?" he asked.

"Probably," she said, bursting out laughing at the thought. "I wasn't exactly a saint in my childhood, but he started it." She heard how that sounded and laughed again.

"I'm not touching that statement with a ten-foot pole. No drawing up sides here," he said.

"Come to think of it, Finn and I used to fight the most," she continued.

"Too close in age?" he asked.

"Probably," she said. "But now he fights fires and our mother couldn't be prouder of him."

They made it to the living room, where Lucas held up his cell. "The marshal just pulled into the driveway."

The driveway was rear-entry, meaning all the houses on this block had their garage doors at the back of the house. It was daylight outside. A sharpshooter could hit them from a good distance on a clear day like today. There were no houses behind them, just a brick wall enclosing the neighborhood and a busy street on the other side of it.

"Are you good?" Ree whispered to Quint.

He nodded before grabbing on to the wall for support. As much as he didn't want to acknowledge it, he would be a liability in a fight right now. But she'd seen bigger healing miracles and figured she'd give him another day to rest and then they'd have a better idea of where he was.

"I'll get A and B," Ree said. The Ivans were inside the second bedroom with the door closed in order to give them privacy. Besides, they didn't have any information that could help the case. Talking to them was fruitless. They were assets to be kept safe and delivered to WITSEC in exchange for information from Axel Ivan.

Ree knocked on the door, then opened it. "Time to go."

Ariana was curled up in her mother's lap. Laurie was stroking her daughter's hair.

"What if we changed our mind and don't want to cooperate?" Laurie asked.

Ree stepped inside the room and closed the door behind her. She moved to the foot of the bed and perched on the edge. "Mind if I ask why?"

The teen whimpered quietly in her mother's arms.

"We've had a change of heart about going along with this." Laurie waved her arms in the air.

"Do you remember what happened in your neighborhood yesterday?" Ree asked.

"I've had a chance to think things over and this isn't the kind of life I want to lead. Always hiding. Running like scared chickens with their heads cut off," Laurie continued as Ariana turned up the tears. "Look at what this is doing to my daughter. She didn't ask for any of this and neither did I."

Ree didn't think this was the exact moment to point out Laurie had, in fact, signed up for this very thing—a husband in jail and a life in hiding. Saying these things out loud wouldn't get her what she wanted or needed—cooperation.

"Let's think this through, Laurie," Ree said in as calm a voice as she could muster. "What happens now if I let you walk out that door?"

"You would do that?" Laurie's surprise would be funny if it wasn't so frustrating. The woman seemed clueless.

"If you refuse to cooperate then you two are the local police's problem, not mine." Ree folded her arms over her chest. Playing a little hardball might work to shock Laurie back to reality.

"What does that mean?" Laurie's eyebrows furrowed.

"Exactly what it sounds like. You walk out the front door and I don't ever see you again," Ree said.

Those words caused Ariana to perk up. She looked up at her mother, big tears spilling down her cheeks. Teenagers sure seemed to know how to pour on the drama and tug at their mother's heartstrings. Growing up with all boys, tears didn't work in the Sheppard household. Ree wouldn't know how to turn hers on. But she had a serious problem sitting a few feet away from her on the bed. Without their cooperation, the investigation died right here. So it was up to her to convince them to stick to the plan.

Chapter Seven

"Mama." There was so much hope and pleading in Ariana's eyes.

"We need to think this through carefully, Ari," Laurie said to her daughter.

Ree was still a little shocked there was anything to think about. "You leave protective custody and there'll be a dozen others coming for you."

Laurie covered her daughter's ears as Ariana buried her head in her mother's arms again. "Please. Not in front of my baby."

This also didn't seem like the time to point out that Ariana was no baby. She was a high-school freshman, which made her around fourteen years old despite looking more mature for her age.

"I'm sorry to be so blunt, Laurie. But I take her life very seriously." Ree figured she needed to take a different approach to get through to these two. "And if I don't inform you of what's likely to happen when you leave without protection, I wouldn't be doing my job. In WITSEC, you'll get the fresh start you need."

The sound of those last words sent Laurie's "baby" into a crying jag. There was only one reason a girl would break down to that degree—a boyfriend.

"I promise you that whoever is in your daughter's life isn't worth risking death for," Ree continued.

The crying ramped up, but Laurie was mulling over the facts. Ree had hit on the teen's reason for working on her mother.

"It's her life, too," Laurie stated with a shrug. "You see how all this is affecting her."

Ree had a suspicion the teen was used to using tears to get what she wanted. It seemed to be working if her mother was considering backing out of WITSEC.

"I have a US Marshal in the house who is expecting to escort both of you to another safe house, where—"

"I can't live in a place like this, Mama," the teen cried in dramatic fashion.

"Do you want to die in a town house?" Ree asked, being as blunt as she could be. The teen needed discipline, not coddling. The best part about Ree's childhood was that she hadn't been sheltered from life, good or bad. Granted, losing her father at such a young age and being brought up in a houseful of testosterone no doubt marked her childhood in a different way. Ree's mother might have wanted a daughter who wore bows in her hair but she would never have tolerated a child who cried to get her way.

On the ranch, everyone had pitched in to clean and do laundry. The boys weren't spared housework and she'd learned to drive the riding lawnmower on her twelfth birthday. Big or small, all ranches operated the same in terms of everyone having to do their part. Big families were no different. The fact that she'd grown up in a big family on a small ranch kept her doubly grounded.

Ariana went all in with the tears.

Laurie started rocking her "baby" and trying to soothe her.

"I know how difficult this must be for both of you. You've been whisked out of your home on a moment's notice and not allowed to bring anything with you but the clothes on your backs. I promise you'll be reunited with a few essentials once you're settled down in a new location," Ree explained.

Crybaby turned it up another notch. How much louder could this teen get? Probably loud enough to get what she wanted. Laurie's face twisted in confusion and what looked like frustration about their predicament.

"It'll be hard at first," Ree continued. "But we're working it out where you'll be able to see your husband on a regular basis."

Laurie perked up over this news.

"I haven't been allowed to visit my Axel in months," she said.

"Your husband asked for these provisions for you and his little girl because he knows the kind of people who want him to keep quiet," Ree continued, figuring she'd struck a nerve. "He claims these same people murdered someone in prison. Do you really believe you and Ariana can go up against them and survive?"

The teen's crying slowed to a whimper with an occasional hiccup.

"Axel is behind bars. How will we ever be safe?" Laurie asked.

"That's a good question," Ree stated. "I'm certain the marshal in the next room can detail out a plan. His agency has been protecting witnesses and their families for a very long time. It's what they specialize in and they are very good at what they do."

"What will happen to my husband?" Laurie asked. At least she seemed concerned about his welfare in all this. Ree was beginning to wonder if the only thing Laurie cared about was her "baby."

"He has already been moved to a different facility and once you're settled, he'll be relocated closer to the two of you so you can see him while he finishes out his sentence rather than go on trial for a crime he didn't commit," Ree said. "I'm not certain all the details of the deal he's asking for but I wouldn't be surprised if a reduced sentence was one of the sticking points."

Laurie looked up and to the left. Ree was getting through to the woman.

"It might be hard at first, but you guys will make new friends while you wait for your husband's release," Ree continued. "Then the three of you will be together again in a new life—a legitimate life where he doesn't have to look over his shoulder to see if his past has caught up with him."

"We'll get new identities?" Laurie asked.

"And so will he," Ree confirmed.

"Mama, we're in love," Ariana whined. "What kind of life do I have without him?"

"You would trade your father for a boyfriend?" Laurie's voice took a different tone now. It reeked of disapproval and the importance of loyalty.

"That's not what I said," Ariana complained.

"Listen to me," Laurie said. "This family means everything to me. We have a chance to be reunited with your father and live together again. Is that something you're willing to trade for a boy?"

Ariana sniffled a couple of times, but her eyes were dry. She might be spoiled and used to getting her way, but she also seemed to realize when she'd overstepped a boundary.

Laurie raised her eyes to meet Ree's.

"You can guarantee I'll see my husband?" she asked.

"I think we both know there are no guarantees in life," Ree said. "Except the fact your allowance will be cut off now that your husband is turning against his former employers."

Laurie's eyes widened.

"Did I forget to mention that earlier?" Ree asked. "Because they'll cut you off financially so quick your head will spin."

Ariana slumped at this news, as though there was a balloon in her chest that had suddenly deflated.

"And that's if they allow you to live, which I sincerely doubt. They will kill you both to get revenge on Axel, who, by the way, asked for nothing for himself except to get to watch his daughter graduate from high school." Ree capitalized on their attention. "Should I send word that you have decided not to follow his wishes to keep you both safe?"

A knock at the door interrupted them. Lucas stuck his head inside.

"The marshal said he doesn't have all day," Lucas said.

"What will it be, ladies?" Ree put the question out there. Now, she had to hope she'd been convincing.

QUINT LEANED AGAINST the wall as Ree led Axel Ivan's family to the living room. Marshal Rodgers has been personally vetted by Bjorn, a reassuring fact. The guy was tall and solidly built.

"Thank you for coming," Ree said to the marshal after shaking hands. No introductions were made with the Ivans. None were necessary. They would be receiving new identities soon enough, anyway. "These are the assets you've been made aware of."

Marshal Rodgers gave a quick nod. "If you ladies will follow me out the back, we'll be on our way."

Mrs. Ivan took in a deep breath, tightening her hold around her daughter. The younger Ivan's face was buried in her mother's arms as they walked out. Mrs. Ivan shot a look at Ree that Quint couldn't quite pinpoint. He crossed his arms over his chest and shifted his gaze to the carpet so as not to make the duo any more uncomfortable.

Ree walked them out the back door and to the garage, disappearing from view when she entered the small hallway that held a washer-and-dryer combo. She returned a few minutes later as the garage door closed.

"What was that all about?" he asked.

"Standing up, I see," she quipped.

"Yes, and you didn't answer my question," he continued.

"They balked about going into WITSEC. I had to talk them into it," she said. "Everything happened so fast back at the town house. I'm guessing they finally had a chance to process and it scared the hell out of them both."

"These things usually involve the opposite sex," he pointed out.

"True enough in this case," she said. "The teenager didn't want to leave her boyfriend. You know what it's like at that age."

"Can't say that I do," he stated. He'd never had a traditional childhood with two parents and gated communities.

"At first, I was afraid Laurie had someone else in her life. I'm not convinced it's untrue, but she seems to be choosing her husband for now," she said.

"He's been away for a couple of years and she was all done up with clothes, hair and makeup," he observed.

"My thoughts exactly when I first saw her. If she's having an affair, the daughter doesn't know," she said. "In the end, Laurie chose her family."

"And we get to fulfill our side of the bargain," Quint said.

Ree nodded.

"Is the interview with Axel set up for tomorrow morning?" he asked.

"I believe so," she stated.

"Do we have a location?" he asked.

"A vehicle will show up at some point tonight with instructions tucked underneath the driver's seat, according to Grappell," she informed him.

"How very Bond of him," Quint joked. He needed to lighten the tension and cracking a joke took his mind off the pain every time he breathed.

"Looks like we have a full day ahead of us," Ree said, quirking an eyebrow as she walked past him. "If that's the best you have, it's going to be a long one."

Ree was out of earshot by the time he came back with a snappy response. He was definitely off his game and had the battle scars to prove it. With nothing to do until early tomorrow morning, he made a couple of loops around the living room and kitchen area before easing down on the sofa, where he put his head back and took a power nap.

He woke to the sounds of *click-click-clack* in the background. Slowly, he brought his hand up to his head and pinched the bridge of his nose. Waiting was torture, but even Quint realized he was in no condition to take anyone on in a physical fight. He also realized he wouldn't exactly be the quickest person right now. All he could count on was a rapid-fire trigger finger. Putting a bullet in someone always was and always would be a last resort. Not only was he bound by a code to uphold the law, but he also believed in it one hundred percent.

Quint blinked a few times. Pain caused his vision to blur. He shook his head. Big mistake there. The movement served to remind him of the headache forming right between his eyes. Since he refused to take any real pain medication, he figured popping a couple ibuprofen would take the edge off enough for him to think a little more clearly.

Normally, a good workout would wipe away at least some of his stress. The point between his shoulder blades felt like someone was stabbing him with a needle. Since push-ups were out of the question, he forced himself to stand up and walk around the room a couple of times. Going outside might be a nice change of scenery, but he would draw attention in his condition.

He glanced around, looking for Ree. She was in the adjacent dining room, sitting across the table from Lucas, who was studying his laptop screen. She had her cell phone out and was typing. Her thumbs moved like lightning.

Seeing her sit with Lucas sent a jolt of jealousy ripping through Quint. After their last conversation, he figured being jealous wasn't productive. They were in a weird place in their relationship where he couldn't move forward or backward. Kissing Ree, making love to her, had been right up there with the best experiences of his life. He'd heard people talk about having a connection with someone like no other and thought it was trying too hard to make something out of thin air. Attraction was a physical response to someone's looks.

Then, he'd met Ree. There was much more to her

than physical beauty. Although, she had that, too. There was a whole lot more to her than intelligence. Although, she had that in spades. And she was an amazing agent—right up there with the best. The connection he had with her, that intangible thing that was almost impossible to explain, was off the charts.

Quint didn't deserve the kind of happiness he could have with Ree. Where was Tessa's happiness? Where was her future? Gone. Erased. Dead.

This damn case might be the death of him, too.

Chapter Eight

"Everything okay?" Ree asked Quint as she watched him pace out of the corner of her eye.

"Sure" was the noncommittal response.

Ree shrugged her shoulders and went back to typing an email to Grappell, trying to get any information out of him she possibly could. It would be helpful if she knew what part of Texas they would be driving to so she could prepare. "Do they have any clothes here besides what's already on your back?"

"Not much." Quint made another lap around the living room. He was still moving slowly but this was an improvement. He was up and around, which was a good sign. She should have known a person as tough as Quint would push himself. Since she would most likely do the same thing if the situation was reversed, she couldn't criticize him.

Tapping her toe on the tile flooring, she waited for a response from Grappell.

"A vehicle has driven by the front of the house for the third time now. I'm watching it from the camera,"

Lucas said, looking up from his laptop and locking gazes with Ree. "This last time, they slowed down."

Ree bit back a curse.

"I didn't do a body check with the teenager like I should have to see if she had a cell phone on her," Ree stated. "I didn't see anything in her hands, so I assumed she'd set it down somewhere inside her house."

"She might have had pockets that weren't easily seen," Lucas said.

"Either way, we're sitting ducks in this house now. We have to move," Ree stated.

"We can take the Jeep in the garage," Lucas said, closing his laptop and tucking it underneath his arm. "I'll give you guys a ride wherever you want to go."

"Let's go," Ree stated, figuring they didn't have much time before the vehicle returned. Her gaze immediately flew to Quint. "Are you good? Do you need help?"

"Never better," he quipped as he beat feet toward her. "Wallet's still in my pocket, so I won't be leaving anything behind."

"Good." Ree moved to his side and helped him toward the hallway leading to the garage.

On the way out, she saw Lucas open a trap door and pull out a case that probably contained weapons.

"What about Chelsea?" she asked.

"She's the one who texted me to take a look at the cameras," Lucas said as he tucked the case that was the size of a decent piece of luggage in the very back of the bright orange Jeep. His Gap T-shirt, cotton shorts and flip-flops were a perfect cover for someone she imagined would drive such a vehicle. There was a Hook 'em Horns bumper sticker on the front of the vehicle. Lucas fit the description of a University of Texas at Austin graduate to a T.

Ree called shotgun, then helped Quint ease into the back seat. Once he was strapped in, settled and armed, she claimed the passenger side.

"Be ready for anything when I hit this button," Lucas said, motioning toward the garage-door release.

"What kind of vehicle am I looking for?" Ree palmed a Glock that had been provided to her when she'd first arrived. She kept the barrel low in the event a neighbor was watching or patrolling the alley out back. Although, this safe house was forever blown at this point. The place would be cleaned out and on the market as arranged by desk-job agents.

"A silver Buick," he stated.

A second later, the button was pushed. The timing couldn't have been worse as the Buick crept along the alley, stopping and blocking them in. The glint of metal had Ree and Lucas both reaching for the button to close the garage door.

As it went down, Quint aimed and fired a shot. "Got a tire and maybe a few extra minutes."

He was already climbing out of the back seat and grimacing with pain that the movement had caused. Ree quickly followed.

"What if you two stay in here and I run around the building?" she asked as an idea took shape. "Get the

Jeep out of the garage and onto the street, where I'll join you."

"Okay," Lucas said. "Go."

Quint's face muscles tensed and she knew he would want to argue.

"There's no time, Quint. Get back inside the vehicle and stick with the plan. I'll back them off. They won't expect me to come from around the house," she stated.

He gave a resigned nod before climbing into the passenger seat. His movement was labored and slow. They both knew he would end up shot, or worse, if he tried to trade places.

Ree threaded her way to the master bedroom, where she opened a window and then climbed out. The hem of her shirt caught on the sill when she jumped. She heard the sound of ripping but would deal with that later.

The door in the eight-foot wooden privacy fence Texans were known for in these parts was locked, so she had to scale it using the Japanese boxwood. Branches jabbed her ankles and calves as she struggled to find her footing.

She scaled the fence, feeling every splinter lodging in her hands and arms. She threw one leg over, then the other, and momentum carried her over the wall. She landed hard on the dry, spiky grass.

Ree popped up to her feet and ran with her Glock out front. The few seconds it took to point and shoot if she didn't have her weapon at the ready could mean the difference between life and death. It was Law Enforcement 101.

The only sound was the hum of the Buick's engine idling in the alleyway behind the home. The driver was waiting. He was about to get a surprise.

The gate leading to the driveway was unlocked. Ree lifted the metal hook and then used her shoulder to keep the gate from closing all the way again. *One. Two. Three.*

She jabbed the door with her shoulder. It swung open. She took aim at the Buick's driver.

The guy had on reflective shades. Since it was lighter outside than inside the Buick, she couldn't get a good look at his face. The only details she could make out were his dark hair and an oval-shaped face. The description narrowed it down to most of the male population in North Texas.

As she squeezed the trigger, the tires spun out and he ducked. The smell of burning rubber lit her nostrils on fire as the Buick jolted forward and out of sight. The garage door slowly opened and then she hopped in the back of the vehicle. Head down, she was ready to fire again. The noise would no doubt draw attention to them.

Lucas bolted out in the opposite direction as Quint stayed on a cell phone. It must belong to Lucas because Quint's had gone missing and a replacement hadn't shown up yet. Ree scanned the area, ready and willing to shoot if their lives were threatened.

She faintly heard Quint providing details of the house's location and the color of the Buick. With a major road behind them, it would be all too easy for him to disappear into traffic. North Dallas was no stranger to traffic jams throughout the day. Even midday, the road was thick with cars as they merged onto Webb Chapel Road.

"Where to?" Lucas finally asked after making a few cuts and unexpected turns. He zipped through traffic with the ease of a native driver. She was used to driving in traffic but never developed a taste for it having grown up in the country.

"Can you get us to Waco?" she asked.

"Don't see why not," Lucas said.

Ree slumped in her seat after buckling the seat belt. "I'll make sure we have a ride from there."

Waco would get her closer to home. For reasons she couldn't explain, she needed to see her house.

BEING INJURED DURING a hot investigation made Quint want to put his fist through a wall.

The ride to Waco was quiet as Ree checked in with Grappell and gave him an update. He arranged for a vehicle to be waiting for them at the parking lot of the $266 million football stadium at Baylor University.

McLane Stadium itself was a sight. It sat on the north bank of the Brazos River, and spectators could arrive by boat.

"Ever been to a game here?" Lucas asked.

"No. You?" Quint asked as the Jeep came to a stop in a parking spot in front of a Chevy Blazer. The vehicle would blend in nicely with drivers on the highway.

"Once, in August, a few years back," Lucas said.

"The season opener?" Quint asked. He kept track of

a few football programs and Baylor University was one of them. Although, it seemed like Alabama's Crimson Tide was an unstoppable force in the game.

"Yup," Lucas said. "Scored tickets through my father, who used to be the special-teams coach."

"Lucky," Quint said, remembering the historic landslide win over SMU.

"It was a great game," Lucas said.

"Did you come in by boat?" Quint asked.

"No, but that would have been epic." Lucas rocked his head and smiled. "Good memories."

"That's about all we can expect in this life, right?" Quint said, wondering where the sudden bout of wistfulness had come from. Had it come out of talking about Tessa earlier with Lucas? For the first time, the memories didn't cut a deeper hole in his heart. The difference was having Ree around. Her presence was a balm on his broken soul. Why couldn't he just go ahead and take the next step with her?

"End of the line," Lucas said. "It's been great working with you both."

"Same with you," Quint said.

"You did great work back there with the unsubs," Lucas said to Ree. "And you saved both of our lives in the driveway. I appreciate it."

"Nothing you wouldn't do for me," Ree said, brushing off the compliment. She always did that a little too quickly.

"Ree is one of the best I've ever had the privilege to work with," Quint said.

"You two are good together," Lucas stated. "It's easy to see."

"A good partnership is built on mutual trust and respect," Ree said quickly. A little too quickly to cover up the fact there'd been more to their relationship than work. Lucas had picked up on it earlier. If he hadn't, he wouldn't be a very observant agent and not someone Quint would feel comfortable working with in the future.

"Yeah," Lucas agreed loosely. His tone said he wouldn't push the issue. "Take care. Both of you."

"Same to you and Chelsea," Ree said.

Quint made his way over to the driver's side and shook Lucas's hand while Ree moved to the Chevy.

"I'd appreciate it if you'd leave the personal stuff out of the case file," Quint said quietly.

"Wouldn't think of adding it," Lucas said, giving Quint a look that said he understood what was really being said.

Quint didn't want anyone to discuss his and Ree's relationship, work or otherwise. He didn't want her name coming up at the proverbial water cooler. In short, he wanted to protect her professional reputation.

"You're a good agent, Lucas," Quint said. "I hope to work with you again someday."

"That means a lot," Lucas responded. "If you need anything, give me a shout. The agency knows how to find me at pretty much all times."

"I swear they put a GPS tracker in all of us during

orientation," Quint quipped, grateful for the lighter conversation.

"Take care of her," Lucas said. "It's obvious to anyone with eyes that she cares a great deal about you, man. Someone like Ree doesn't come around often."

"I will," Quint promised. "And I hear you."

The statement made Quint realize he wasn't the only one interested in her. It seemed Lucas had noticed her, too. Maybe Quint's earlier jealousy wasn't so far-fetched after all.

The sun was blazing by the time Lucas pulled away. Quint had a headache to match. Ree had gone to the back tire on the driver's side to retrieve the key.

"Where are we headed?" he asked, because it was clear she had a destination in mind.

"I need to go home," she said, giving him a look that told him not to argue.

"Let's go home then," he stated without hesitation.

"I let Grappell know. He said we'd be safe to get to our next destination by ten o'clock tomorrow," she said as she climbed into the driver's seat. "Do you need a hand up?"

"No," he replied. "I got this."

The pain was real as he reached for the handle and pulled himself up while taking a step on the stair that came out as soon as he opened the door. At least Grappell had sprung for a deluxe model. Quint would give him that.

"Any chance you have ibuprofen at your house?" Quint asked after a while.

"That, and coffee," she said, ramping up the speed on the highway.

"Mind if I lean back while you drive?" he asked, figuring he could get in a catnap so he'd be fresh by the time they got to her house. *Fresh* was a relative term considering he hadn't showered in the past twenty-four hours.

"Go for it," she said with a shrug.

He couldn't quite pinpoint what had changed in her during the last couple of hours. They'd been in rough spots before and gotten out just fine. They'd been shaken up before and she'd kept her eye on the prize. Granted, they were technically in between assignments at the moment. Going home and freshening up was probably a good idea. They'd lost everything they'd had with them, anyway.

At her place, they could regroup and maybe get in a full eight hours of sleep before heading out to wherever Axel was being transported. All Quint knew was they'd delivered the wife and kid. Their part of the deal was done. There was no reason for Axel to withhold names now.

That was Quint's last thought before he dozed off. By the time he woke, Ree was gently shaking him by the shoulder.

"Hey, sleepyhead. We're here," she said. She'd managed to park, turn off the vehicle and come around to the passenger side without disturbing him. That must be some kind of record. It also spoke to the injuries Quint had racked up. He never slept so deeply that the slightest noise didn't wake him.

He'd needed the sleep, though.

"That was fast," he teased.

"Easy for you to say." She rolled her eyes and smiled. The day had been long already and it was barely dinnertime.

Quint forced himself out of the Chevy and followed her to the front door. "Did Grappell give you any idea where we'll be going tomorrow morning for the meeting?"

"None. They struck a deal to release Axel now that someone came forward to corroborate his story, so they are working out the details of what that will look like," she said, unlocking and opening her door. The lights were on, so she held a hand up.

Quint pulled the borrowed Glock out of his holster, ready to clear the place. Neither spoke as they moved with precision through the living room, weapons leading the way. After the living room, dining room and kitchen were cleared, Ree led him to the hallway. She took two steps in and stopped.

The bathroom door was cracked open. Apparently, this wasn't something that normally happened at Ree's house. She put up a fisted hand as a warning.

Quint took in a slow breath, wondering if this day was about to get a whole lot worse.

Chapter Nine

Ree's finger hovered over the trigger mechanism. This seemed to be turning into one of those days. Hell, this case was turning into one of those cases that never seemed to end and kept getting worse. If she didn't care so much about Quint, she would have pulled out. It had bad juju all over it and she should probably run as far away as possible.

Sticking with the case was the only way to ensure Quint would be all right. She couldn't let him be assigned a random partner who wouldn't understand him because he wouldn't abandon her, either, when times got tough.

The wood flooring creaked right before the bathroom door opened and Zoey yelled, "Surprise!"

Ree blew out a sharp breath as she considered just how close Zoey had come to having her head blown off.

"Sorry." Zoey's big brown eyes widened as fear seemed to strike a physical blow. She was holding the cutest golden retriever puppy in her arms. "I got a dog."

"Where are you parked?" Ree asked, trying to shake

out of the fog. Zoey York was a young woman Ree had met during the Greenlight bust. She'd been caught up in a bad relationship that nearly cost her everything. Ree was able to convince Zoey to get help in a women's shelter in Austin.

Quint had lowered his weapon and placed a hand on her shoulder. His touch was reassuring despite the fact she didn't want it to be.

"You scared me to death," Zoey said, her shoulders dropping as she walked straight up to Ree and brought her into a hug.

"I didn't know you were here," Ree said, hoping she and Quint hadn't just given away the fact they worked in law enforcement.

"You asked about my car. I parked around back because I wanted to surprise you," Zoey said.

"How'd you get in?" Ree asked, then realized this wasn't the first time Zoey had broken in somewhere. The eighteen-year-old had slipped into the cabin during Quint and Ree's first case in Cricket Creek, Texas.

"I let myself in," Zoey said with a smile. She had a mischievous twinkle in her eyes. "Hi, Quint."

"How long have you been here?" Ree asked, turning tail and walking into the living room. The others followed.

"Twenty minutes," Zoey said.

"Why aren't you still at the shelter?" Ree asked, motioning toward the small round dining table adjacent to the kitchen.

"I'm out on furlough and I didn't have any place to go, so..."

"Don't mind me. I need a shower," Quint said.

"What happened to you?" Zoey looked him up and down.

"I got into a motorcycle accident," he said.

"Oh, no." Zoey's face morphed to concern.

"I'll be fine," Quint reassured her. "You two catch up while I get cleaned up."

"How did you find this place?" Ree asked, hoping their cover wasn't blown. Zoey would believe that she and Quint were newlyweds. She also just realized Quint wasn't wearing the boot that had also been part of their cover story. Although, weeks had passed since the first case and he could technically be out of the boot by now.

"You sent flowers. Thank you, by the way." Zoey shrugged. She really was a resourceful young person. "I met a genius hacker in Austin and she got the address from the florist's database."

"Remind me never to be on your bad side," Ree teased.

"You couldn't be," Zoey said so fast and with innocence that tugged at Ree's heart.

"How are you doing? Really?" Ree asked, moving to the coffee machine. She'd hoped for a few hours of rest but seeing Zoey again was providing a different kind of moral boost.

Zoey had gotten herself involved in an abusive relationship. One of the best things that had come out of the

Cricket Creek bust was that Ree had convinced Zoey to go to a women's shelter in Austin.

"It's only been a few weeks, so this is going to sound stupid, but I can already feel a difference," Zoey said, her brown eyes lighting up when she spoke. "Week one, I was a hot mess. The second week wasn't much better, but then something clicked inside me around the third week that asked what kind of person I wanted to be and what kind of relationship I wanted to be in. I'd honestly never asked myself those questions before."

"Did you find answers?" Ree asked, going about fixing the coffee.

"Yes. I want to be like you," Zoey said. Her answer pretty much melted Ree's heart. Zoey was a good and decent young woman who deserved more than the hand she'd been dealt in life, with a mother who'd ditched her daughter. There'd been no one to care about Zoey, and she'd gotten mixed up with the wrong person.

"That's quite a compliment," Ree said. They were racking up today. "One I appreciate very much."

Zoey practically beamed as Ree poured two cups of coffee and brought one over. She set it down on the table in front of Zoey.

"I'd like to be more like you, too," Ree admitted.

Zoey's face twisted up in confusion.

"You're smart and kind. You're a really good person who is working hard to better yourself," Ree stated. "Plus, you really know how to break into a place."

Zoey laughed.

Ree also made a mental note to get an alarm system

installed. She'd never really thought about one before, since she'd lived in the country. Most folks kept their doors unlocked and their vehicles running when they popped out to the store for a quick errand. The thought of an alarm was the last thing on Ree's mind despite working a job most would consider dangerous.

Thankfully, there wasn't a whole lot of agency paraphernalia lying around. Ree had decorated with a few random snapshots of her and her brothers. Her mother was in a picture or two with Ree's father before their world had been turned upside down by his death. And then there was a picture of Ree's grandfather, whom she adored. She'd been worried about him while in Houston and the worry turned out to be for nothing. He was fine, same as always.

It occurred to Ree the jig might be up on the marriage front, considering Quint didn't have any clothes hanging in the closet and Zoey struck Ree as the type who might snoop around if she got bored. However, there had to be something of one of her brothers around.

And then she realized what she had. A smile turned up the corners of her lips when she held up a finger and said she'd be right back.

Ree made a beeline for her master bedroom closet. Voila! There it was, folded and on top of the vintage dresser inside her walk-in. Overalls made from denim no less. She grabbed them, along with a T-shirt and boxers she'd washed after her brother had taken a fall in the mud while helping her install gutters six months ago.

She knocked on the bathroom door before walking

inside. The water was running and the outline of Quint's strong frame came through the white curtain.

"I found clothes for you to wear since I realized you don't have anything here. I don't think Zoey is on to us but she will be if she realizes you don't have clothes in the same house you're supposed to live in," Ree said. She heard her own voice and tried to clear the frog in her throat.

The spigot squeaked before the water turned off. Suddenly Ree wasn't laughing. Instead, her heart raced as her pulse kicked up a few notches. Quint ripped open the curtain and stood there with a towel wrapped around his waist, wad of Saran wrap in his hand. Beads of water rolled down a muscled chest and onto a bandaged stomach. She set down the folded clothing on the counter and backed out of the room.

"Thank you," Quint said, drying his hair with a different towel. Lucky towels, she thought.

"I'll just be in the other room if you need anything else," she said, thinking how easy it was to lean into her attraction to Quint and how hard reality was when it slapped her in the face.

Before he could answer or she could say anything she might regret, she turned and headed back to the living room, where Zoey waited.

QUINT STOOD THERE, drying off, forcing his thoughts away from Ree and back onto the case. There was at least a slight chance Axel's wife and daughter might renege on their promise to go into WITSEC. He wouldn't rest easy until they got the information from Axel as promised and it checked out.

Hunger pangs had him moving a little faster than his injuries would have liked, but the smell of food wafting down the hallway made him realize how long it had been since he'd eaten.

Quint picked up the denim overalls and shook his head. This would have to do even though it would make him look like Farmer Brown. At least the items were clean. The T-shirt wasn't bad. It fit a little tight, but he could make do. The boxers were a little snug as well, but clean trumped fitted or anything else right now.

As he dressed, he checked his bandages. They seemed to be holding despite the shower. He wasn't looking forward to changing them considering the hairs on his chest would be yanked out along with the tape holding him together.

The sleep on the way over made a dent in how Quint was feeling. If he could just cocoon for a couple of days, he'd be good to go. Since they didn't have the luxury, he'd do what he could.

Overalls on, he headed down the hallway and to the kitchen. He heard the low hum of conversation and the lighthearted laughter Ree deserved. He was beginning to feel like he was bringing nothing but destruction and sorrow to Ree's life.

Quint stopped himself right there. Ree was a solid agent. He would put her skills up against the best and she would come out on top. She'd chosen this life, this job. And yet, he couldn't deny there was something different about her now. From the day he'd met her on the first case to now, there'd been a subtle shift and he couldn't quite put his finger on what had caused it.

"What's cooking?" he said as he came around and into view.

"Pizza," Ree said. "I have one with the works on now and there's a barbecue-chicken one up next. Take your pick."

A bell dinged and he assumed it meant the pizza was done cooking.

"I'll take the first available," he quipped before catching Zoey eyeing him up and down. She was savvy and would have questions. This time, he didn't have any easy explanations, so he decided to avoid any potential land-mine topics altogether.

Ree had three plates stacked by the pizza cooker sitting on the counter. She sliced the pizza before placing the second one in the fancy cooker with a rotating heating element. He had an oven and a microwave at his place. Those were the only two places any cooking or heating got done. He could admit to mostly heating. Ree, he'd noticed, had all kinds of small appliances. She had a blender on the countertop for one. And a toaster. She definitely had more than two pans in her cupboard.

She portioned out three slices on each plate as he joined her.

"I can take these two," he said, picking up his and Zoey's plates.

"Okay," she said. "I'll grab drinks."

"Nothing but water for me," he said. "And I'll grab my own."

When he turned, he caught Zoey staring at them with her mouth open.

"What?" he asked as he brought over the two plates.

"Nothing." She shrugged before fixing her gaze on the plate in front of her. "I've just never seen that before."

"Never seen what?" he asked, taking a seat at the cozy table.

"A man help around the kitchen," she said as her cheeks turned three shades of red from embarrassment. She stroked the puppy in her lap double time.

"Everyone should pitch in," he stated, picking up a hot slice and then quickly setting it back down. "I grew up with a single mother. My dad ditched us before I had a chance to get to know him. My head wasn't on straight for a long time and I gave her hell, which I'm not proud of to this day. When I finally woke up to what a jerk I was being, I figured it was up to me to find ways to make her life easier, not harder. After that, I paid attention in school and brought my grades up. I stopped getting in fights and hanging around with the wrong crowd. And I didn't wait for her to ask me to take out the trash or help set the table."

A hint of a smile crossed the young woman's face.

"That's nice," she said. "The part about you deciding to help out."

"It's what I should have done all along but didn't," he said.

"Where is your mother now?" Zoey asked, picking up a slice as Ree joined them.

"She passed away years ago," he said before getting hit with a surprising bout of melancholy. He could be honest with himself enough to admit he still missed her. It was worse some days more than others. He could only hope his mother was looking after Tessa and her baby in a better place.

Although they'd never met, he had always believed his mother would have gotten along well with Tessa. And she would have loved Ree. Quint stopped himself right there before he let himself go down that road.

"I'm sorry," Zoey said. "That must have been hard on you since the two of you were so close."

He nodded.

"At least she got to see her son turn his life around," he said. "I think that's all she wanted in the end. Just to see me doing well and being a decent human being."

Zoey smiled but it didn't reach her eyes.

"My mom ditched like your dad," she said after taking a bite of pizza. "It's probably for the best."

The pain in her voice nearly gutted him. She was too young to be all alone with no one to help guide her. He needed to change the subject before he got angry at Zoey's lot in life.

"What's her name?" He motioned toward the dog in her lap.

"I haven't decided yet," she said, perking up considerably. "Let me know if you have any ideas."

"Maggie," he said.

Zoey wrinkled her forehead. "No. It doesn't fit."

"Dixie?"

She shook her head.

"Marley?" he continued, unfazed.

"Too sad," she quickly countered.

"You're probably right about that one," he laughed before taking another bite. "Molly?"

"What's up with all these names that begin with the letter *M*?" Zoey asked.

"Piper?" he continued.

Zoey thought about that one for a long moment before nixing it, too.

"Your food is getting cold," Ree scolded.

The three of them sitting here like this, bantering back and forth about names, caused an ache to form in Quint's chest. Out of the blue, he wondered what it would be like to sit here with his and Ree's kid and a dog.

Chapter Ten

"Pixie."

Ree laughed at how determined Quint seemed to be to find the perfect name for Zoey's dog. Her cell buzzed, indicating a text coming through. She excused herself and went over to the coffee table, where she remembered last setting it down.

The message was from Agent Grappell. There was an address along with confirmation of the meetup time. She looked up the address on the map feature and saw that it was a residence on Lake Travis in Austin and not a jail. Interesting. The only reason she could think of was that it would be too dangerous to keep Axel locked up in any institution. Dumitru's reach was shocking if that was true. Then again, Bjorn might not want to take any chances. She could be dotting every *i* and crossing every *t*. He was also going to testify against someone in law enforcement who killed a prisoner.

Axel was in a no-win situation. At least he would be reunited with his wife and daughter in the process.

Sitting at the table with Quint, Zoey and the dog had

put a different image in her thoughts. She'd locked gazes with Quint at one point and, for a split second, could have sworn he was thinking the exact same thing. But kids and a dog weren't something she'd ever seen herself wanting. What had changed?

Ree could admit to feeling a certain emptiness in her life. The fact her mother constantly seemed eager to push Ree's buttons made her want to run in the opposite direction. She sighed and then rejoined the other two at the table.

"Ruby?" Quint asked.

Zoey laughed and held the puppy even closer to her chest. "I just don't see her as a Ruby. You know?"

"Sandy?" he continued.

"How about Red?" Zoey said with the excitement of a six-year-old on Christmas morning.

"I mean if you want a plain name that's more of a description than anything else...fine." Quint crossed his arms over his chest and made a pouty face.

Ree was probably just exhausted, but she broke out into a stomach-busting laugh. The kind that made her double over and went on so long her cheeks actually hurt. How long had it been since she'd really laughed?

In that moment, she realized she had some thinking to do about her life, her next steps and her future. If the thought of having a dog made her happy, she should go for it. Would she miss going undercover? Living on the edge?

This job was the only thing she'd known. She'd gone to work for the ATF immediately out of college. She'd only ever wanted to work in law enforcement and had never considered any other possibility. At thirty-six, she was also starting to realize there were other things in life she'd given up in order to have the career she'd wanted.

Looking at Red made her heart hurt. She could see a puppy running around on her small property, constantly by her side. A flash of a kiddo sitting in a high chair, dropping pieces of food as scraps and laughing furiously when the dog snapped them up.

This seemed like a good time to remind herself near-death experiences had a way of causing a person to reexamine life choices. This wasn't the first time she'd reevaluated going all in with her career and leaving almost no room for anything else. It was just the first time the idea had any teeth to it.

After two pizzas were inhaled, the trio took the dog out back for a walk. Ree arranged for her brother Shane to take care of having an alarm installed while she was in Austin the following morning. The faster she got that extra layer of protection, the better, as far as she was concerned. There was something particularly creepy about this case. It was probably the prison murders and the fact they were having to take so many precautions with Axel.

If Zoey could get inside Ree's home, someone else could, too. Shane texted back that he could get her remote monitoring with the ability to turn the alarm on and off with her smartphone. The idea appealed even more. Technology was a miracle when it wasn't being a pain in the backside. She couldn't imagine living without her cell phone. The thought of being away from it even for a few hours gave her anxiety. She had no idea how Quint was surviving.

The walk around her property had done her good. Now, Quint sat on the grass, playing with Red. Zoey looked more like her age than Ree had ever seen. Pride welled up in her chest at the progress Zoey was making in her life. Being able to help someone like her was a rewarding part of the job.

Strangely, there was less helping in that sense and more locking bad guys away so they couldn't hurt anyone else. Knowing her efforts protected people like Zoey gave her a deep sense of pride. The only problem was how easy it became to lose sight of what was important when she constantly dealt with the dark side of humanity.

Watching Zoey, Ree realized she wanted to work more with young people like her. People who'd had a bad draw in the form of parents. There were too many folks who didn't have a person in the world who seemed to care about them.

The urge to do more about it struck. Ree would let the idea sit for a minute and see if it gained any steam.

Zoey pushed up to standing and gathered her puppy in her arms. "I have to drive back now. There's a ten-o'clock curfew."

"The shelter is okay with you having Red?" Ree asked. She had been wanting to foster a puppy for when

Zoey left the shelter and got established on her own somewhere but didn't have time.

"I got it okayed by my case worker," she said with a smile. It was good to see her happy. She really was a sweetheart. *Bad break*, Ree thought.

Despite her constant conflicts with her mother, Ree could honestly say she never doubted the woman loved her. Ree also had brothers and a grandfather who would do anything for her. She glanced at Zoey and then Quint. He'd had a mother who loved him, at least. He'd had someone who believed in him and became a father figure. Families weren't always created by birth. She thought about the sister-brother love Quint and Tessa had shared and how that bond was still very much alive even though Tessa was gone. Some families came from the heart instead.

"It's really good to see you, Zoey." Ree hugged the puppy and young woman in one fell swoop.

Quint managed to stand up on his own with some effort. It took him a second and pain was written all over his face, but he smiled and winked in acknowledgment of his progress.

"Drive safe on your way back to Austin," Ree said as Zoey climbed in her two-door blue hatchback.

Ree stuck out her hand.

"Hand me your phone," she said.

Zoey gave a confused look but complied with the request.

"I'm putting my number in here," Ree stated as she tapped away at the screen. "The next time you want to visit, make sure you text first in case I'm not home. I have an alarm company coming tomorrow and you won't be able to break in any longer."

Ree handed over the cell when she was done.

"Will do," Zoey said, looking like a scolded teenager. Red bounced around in his box in the passenger seat. "Simmer down, Red."

"Let Ree know if you need anything, Zoey," Quint said. "I mean it."

"Stop by if you're ever in Austin," Zoey said.

"You know we will," Ree said. "I texted myself using your phone so I have your number now, too."

Zoey cranked up the engine with a wide smile. There was something different about her that was hard to pinpoint. There was a spark in her eyes now.

Had Ree lost the spark in hers?

"BED" WAS ALL Quint said as he watched Zoey take off, her blue hatchback disappearing around the bend.

"I was thinking the same thing," Ree admitted. "You've already showered, so you're ahead of the game."

"What was the text about earlier?" Quint asked.

"Grappell was confirming the time for the meetup and he sent an address in Austin," she stated.

"Doesn't look like we'll be dropping by to see Zoey on this trip," Quint said, taking her hand and tugging her inside the house. He locked up behind them as Ree cleared the dishes from the table. The two worked in comfortable silence. Neither of them needed to fill the air with words, plus Quint didn't have the energy to do a whole lot of talking, anyway.

"This is the second time she's broken in somewhere we were staying," Ree said when they met at the mouth of the hallway. "And this time, it was my house."

"You weren't kidding about the alarm, were you?" he asked.

"No. I can't be caught off guard like that again," she stated. "Zoey reminded me that my place is vulnerable and it shouldn't be."

Quint nodded.

"Where do you want me?" he asked, motioning toward the hallway.

"Since I'm repainting my guest bedroom and it's a mess right now, you'll have to sleep with me in the master," she said, a sexy red blush crawling up her neck.

"I can make do on the sofa if that's better," he offered if it would make her more comfortable.

"You'll sleep a whole lot better on my bed. It's comfortable and you're way too big to fit on my sofa. Be real, Quint." Ree rolled her eyes and then laughed. "I'm slap-happy. I'm probably not going to make a whole lot of sense from here on out. But I have an extra toothbrush still in its wrapper in my medicine cabinet that you're welcome to have."

"Already beat you to that one," he said. "I couldn't stand my breath and thought it was criminal to force it on you and Zoey."

Ree laughed again before straightening up. "I'm

going to take a shower. My bedroom has blackout curtains. You're welcome to close them."

"I like to know when the sun comes up, if that's all right with you," he said.

"Same. I used to use them a long time ago and then stopped because I felt like I was in a cave and had no idea when it was night or day," she stated, then pointed toward the master before heading that way.

Quint went around the place, double-checking window locks and then doors. When Ree's home was safely secured, he made a beeline for the master bath. Ignoring the fact Ree was naked behind the curtain, he brushed his teeth before hitting the sack. His eyes were barely closed when he conked out...

An alarm shrieked. Quint bolted upright. The sun peeking through the slats of the miniblinds told him it was time to be awake.

Ree absently reached over and tapped at the alarm, no doubt trying to find the snooze button. He moved around to her side of the bed and turned off the noise instead. She groaned. "Time to get up already?"

"We had a solid ten hours of sleep," he said quietly, liking the fact she'd been curled up next to him in bed all night. He cursed himself for not bringing in the suitcase. What was wrong with him? Ree was the only person he'd ever wanted to bring a suitcase to and yet he'd stopped himself.

Before he chewed on that again, he figured the least he could do was make coffee before she got out of bed. Thankfully, he'd peeled himself out of those overalls last night. The boxers might be a little bit tight but the seams weren't busting out. He wished he hadn't left the suitcase in his vehicle for more than one reason.

As Quint fumbled around looking for coffee supplies, he heard a key being inserted into the lock in the living room.

"Hey, sis." Shane's voice was unmistakable. And since he was in the living room, there was no way Quint was getting out of being caught in his underwear in the kitchen.

Since he didn't want to surprise Shane, Quint cleared his throat. "She's in the bedroom. I'm making coffee. How about a cup?"

"Quint?" Shane didn't bother to hide his shock.

"It's me," Quint confirmed.

"I thought the alarm contractor might have beaten me here," Shane said in exacerbation as he rounded the corner, then stopped cold in his tracks. He gave Quint a once-over before taking a step back.

"My clothes are in the next room," Quint said, pouring a cup of fresh brew. "Coffee?"

"Thanks," Shane said, taking the offering but looking mighty unsure of this situation.

"We're working a case together and I got into a fight," Quint stated as he poured his own cup and one for Ree.

"I hope the other guy looks worse," Shane quipped. They both laughed. It was to relieve some of the awkward tension of Shane walking into his sister's house to find a man in her kitchen who was barely dressed.

The alarm in the master blared again.

"I'll just take this to Ree and throw on some pants," Quint said.

"Sounds like a plan." Shane turned toward the window as Quint walked past.

Ree was wrestling with the alarm clock when Quint returned.

"Hey, you might want to get up seeing as how your brother is here." Quint looked around for the overalls he'd shed last night before climbing in bed.

"Shane is here?" Ree sat right up after hearing that news.

"He's in the kitchen, drinking coffee," Quint said, taking a sip of fresh brew before setting his mug on top of the dresser. He located the overalls and pulled them on, thinking he should have thrown his clothes in the wash yesterday. He'd been preoccupied nursing his injuries.

"What did he say?" Ree asked, throwing covers off and scrambling out of bed.

"That he was going outside to get his shotgun," Quint joked.

Ree's expression was priceless. The moment of shock before she realized he was jerking her chain was worth the pain that came with laughing.

"For that, I'm not giving your other clothes back," she stated.

"Even though I brought coffee?" he asked, motioning toward the mug he'd set next to her side of the bed on the nightstand.

"Have I told you how much I love you?" Ree's expression dropped the instant those words left her mouth. She immediately started backtracking. "I wasn't saying that I—"

"Don't worry about it," he interjected. "It's just an expression. I knew what you meant."

"That's a relief," she said before taking a sip of coffee. She lifted the mug in the air afterward. "Remind me not to talk before I've had a sufficient amount of caffeine in the future, will you?"

Quint wasn't so sure he wanted to take that bargain. Hearing the words *I love you* come out of Ree's mouth had caused his chest to squeeze.

Chapter Eleven

Ree threw on clothes, brushed her teeth and polished off her first cup of coffee for the day before deciding to face her brother. She'd packed an overnight bag while Quint had been asleep last night, so she brought that out to the living room and set it next to the door before getting a yogurt from the fridge.

Thankfully, Shane was outside with the alarm-company contractor. She wanted to slip out the door and head to Austin without having a big conversation with her brother about something she couldn't exactly define. Her relationship with Quint was professional only. Everything else between them was complicated and she didn't know how to define it, let alone explain it to someone else.

So when Quint was fed, caffeinated and dressed before Shane came back inside, she was relieved.

"Ready?" she asked. "We'll be late if we don't get out of here right now."

"Don't you want to speak to Shane?" Quint asked.

"No," she said quickly. A little too quickly?

Ree shook her head and then grabbed her overnight bag. She slipped the strap over her shoulder. "Bjorn approved a clothing allowance for you since you can't exactly wear the same outfit every day you borrowed from the safe house, but, fair warning, she didn't give a whole lot." She cracked a smile at the thought of him shopping in a thrift store. "We could probably hit an army surplus store on the way to Austin."

"Funny," he said, heading toward the door with a piece of toast in his hand. "We'll be able to stop off at my place after the meetup."

"You don't live far from Austin?" she asked.

He shook his head. "New Braunfels area."

"Okay then," she said. "Shall we see what Axel Ivan has to say?"

"After all the trouble we went through to ensure his wife and daughter are safe, he'd better have something we can use," Quint muttered under his breath.

Ree couldn't agree more. Axel's family had been a handful and his teenager had most likely been responsible for ruining a safe-house location in the process. Teens and their phones. Ree understood how lost she'd feel without hers. And yet, if it came down to life or death, she'd have no problem ditching her cell.

Leading the way outside, she ducked when Shane tried to wave her over.

"Gotta run," she shouted as she tossed her overnight bag in the back seat before climbing into the driver's seat of the Chevy.

Shane looked a little constipated, like he had a whole lot to say and the words were backed up.

"I'll call you later," she said, then closed the door and started the engine.

"You're sure getting out of Dodge a little fast," Quint stated as he eased into the passenger seat.

"My brother walked in on you in my kitchen wearing nothing but boxers that didn't leave a whole lot to the imagination," she said as she stomped on the gas pedal. "What do *you* think he wants to talk to me about? It sure isn't the alarm system."

"Oh," Quint said.

"'Oh' is right," she agreed before navigating onto the main road and then the highway. The steady hum of tires on pavement was the only noise in the vehicle on the way to the meetup.

"Where exactly are we headed again?" Quint asked, breaking the silence.

"It's a house overlooking Lake Travis," she said. "I mapped it out earlier and the turnoff is easy to miss. It comes not long after a corner store and is basically vertical for a quarter of a mile."

"I can drive if it's a problem for you," he offered.

"Thanks, but you seem to keep forgetting that I grew up with four brothers who kept me on my toes," she said. "Plus, we're still in the heat of Texas. It's not like there will be ice or anything to worry about."

"True."

Ree continued the drive in silence until they passed

the corner store. "There's the road we're looking for. If you can call it that."

It wasn't even a paved road so she was grateful for the SUV. There was only one way to get up that hill, and that was to go for it. Hesitate and she'd lose traction. It was a whole lot like driving on ice in that respect. She had to move at a slow and steady pace.

Gravel spewed underneath tires as she snaked up the trail. She was never more thankful than when the road leveled off and resembled something like tar. She didn't realize how stressed she'd been until she glanced at the rearview mirror and saw beads of sweat on her forehead.

Thankful that was over, she finished the drive and parked in the driveway of the safe house. There had to be cameras in the trees on the way up to the home. No one could drive a vehicle up here and go undetected.

"Let's do this," Quint said, seeming eager to get out of the Chevy.

Before they exited the vehicle, a man in a dark suit walked out. His tie was undone and he had an earpiece.

"My name is Marshal Hamlin." He immediately stuck his hand in between him and Quint, who happened to be closest to the door. Quint eased the rest of the way out of the SUV and took the offering.

"I'm Agent Casey and this is my partner Agent Shepperd," Quint said.

Hamlin met Ree in front of the SUV for a vigorous shake. After exchanging pleasantries, his face morphed into a serious expression. “As you both know, the implications in this case make it more sensitive than most.”

“We’re aware,” Ree said.

“I’ll have to check your IDs and pat you down. No weapons are allowed inside,” Hamlin continued.

Ree didn’t like the sound of that, but she could see where a criminal could take advantage of an armed agent if they lost focus. She wouldn’t argue and shot a look at Quint when he started to. WITSEC was the US Marshals Service territory. It wasn’t her and Quint’s place to question their protocol.

Quint pulled out his wallet and showed his license. Ree did the same. When Hamlin had checked both, inspecting them like he was a customs agent and they were trying to get back in the country, he nodded.

“I apologize for any inconvenience,” he said, motioning for them to put their hands on the hood of the Chevy.

“I’ll save you the trouble,” Ree stated. “I’m armed.” She pulled her Glock out of the holster underneath her armpit and placed it under the seat of the Chevy. Quint did the same with his weapon.

“I still have to pat you down,” Hamlin informed them.

Ree put out her hands and positioned her legs three feet apart. Quint followed suit but the look on his face told her phone calls were going to be made after they walked out of this house.

QUINT OPENED THE door for Ree, needing something to do with his hands besides throw a punch at the arrogant agent who'd just patted down him and Ree. Hamlin had known to expect them and, no doubt, had personally watched them drive up the road on camera. He'd probably also used facial-recognition software to ensure it was truly them. The pat-down was wholly unnecessary in Quint's book. Hamlin was flexing, saying he was in charge.

Since all Quint needed from Axel was a name and a trail to follow, he brushed off his frustration.

"Thank you," Ree said as she crossed over the threshold.

He gave a quick nod and could see she was reading him. She would also realize his laser focus was engaged. Following her inside, the hallway was dark despite the time. They'd been punctual, too, arriving at 9:53 a.m. The dark wood flooring extended down a set of five steps where the room opened up to what might look like a small art gallery. Two crushed-velvet sofas faced each other, acting as the center point of the room. The walls had dim lights illuminating various pieces of artwork, most of which was centered around photographs of nature and trees.

Another set of five stairs down and the rather large rectangular dining room seated a dozen folks. There was half the number currently engaged in conversation. Coffee mugs in a neat line. The entire home was positioned to take advantage of the wall of windows and the view of treetops perched above the lake.

The place looked like something out of *Architectural Digest* magazine. It might not be Quint's personal taste, but it was a piece of art. This was by far the fanciest safe house Quint had ever seen and he wondered what kind of favors had been called in to get this place. He also couldn't help wondering who owned the place.

As the trio made their way toward the table, a few glances came their way. No one seemed to be bothered by their presence or feel threatened. But then Hamlin did a decent job of screening as annoying as the man could be.

A person who had his back to the room was large-framed enough to be Axel. His dark hair was cut short, curling just above the collar. He wore a crisp white tailored shirt.

Ree and Quint joined the small group at the table after a quick introduction by Hamlin. Other than Axel, there were five agents present. There were three males, plus Hamlin, and two females, representing three agencies. Now Quint understood why Axel wasn't in prison. He was giving up names, dates and locations. He had to be in order to have this many law-enforcement personnel in one room ready and waiting to interview him.

"Now that the final two agents are here, why don't you start from the beginning and tell everyone what happened in the prison yard that day," one of the male agents sitting at the head of the table said.

Hamlin immediately disappeared once they sat.

"Once this meeting is done, I'll be reunited with my family?" Axel asked as he took a seat.

"We've gone over this before, sir," the lead agent said. "The answer is still the same. Give us enough information and you'll get to be with your family again. The three of you will then leave with Marshal Hamlin."

Axel nodded. He was a large man with the kind of build people referred to as big-boned. His short haircut did little to veil an oversize forehead. His large nose hooked and he had the kind of pockmarked skin that revealed he'd struggled with acne in his teenage years. Still, there was a particular refinement about the way he sat there, in his tailored shirt and black slacks, hands folded on top of the table.

Would he give Quint and Ree the information they needed?

Chapter Twelve

Ree leaned back in her chair with her back facing the incredible view of treetops and the lake beyond. She crossed her arms over her chest and studied Axel Ivan. After meeting his wife and daughter, she tried to fit the puzzle pieces together. She thought about the possibility of Laurie Ivan having an affair while her husband was incarcerated. The man sitting across the table wasn't the type to take an affair lightly.

For Laurie's sake, she hoped Axel never found out.

"It went down like this," Axel said, the grip on his hands tightening. "Correction Officer Ricky Barns came to my cell one night. He stood on the other side of the bars and tapped his billy club against the metal until I woke up. It was the middle of the night." He shrugged. "I'm not sure exactly what time but it was pitch-black outside."

He glanced at the faces around the table. Was he gauging whether or not each agent believed him so far?

"He mumbled something about it being my unlucky day," Axel continued when no one spoke. "I asked him what he was talking about but all he said was that my number had come up. He threw me for a loop because on the inside certain groups look out for their own. You know what I mean?"

A few heads nodded. One of the agents was recording the session. Others nursed cups of coffee as they studied Axel. Everyone at the table was getting a read on the man and she hoped they would exchange notes at the end of the interview.

"Sure," the lead agent said.

"So I couldn't figure out what the hell Ricky—"

Axel looked around like he'd just given out the secret recipe to Coke. When he was satisfied no one seemed upset by the familiarity of using the officer's first name, he kept going. "The man says something that stuck with me next. He said he was unlucky, too. Said we were two unlucky bastards." Axel stopped like he needed a minute before continuing. "Then he walks off like I'm supposed to know what any of that means."

"And what did it mean?" the lead agent asked.

"That I was going down for murder and Ricky was the one who got tagged to do it," Axel said as a thin sheen of sweat covered his Frankenstein-like forehead. His pulse seemed to kick up a few notches at recounting the story and he shifted positions in his seat, as if he was suddenly uncomfortable.

"How do you know it was Officer Barns who killed the victim?" the lead agent continued.

"I stayed up after his visit and tried to figure out what he meant," Axel admitted. "When I tried to go back to sleep, my eyes wouldn't stay shut. After that, I paid attention when Officer Barns interacted with anyone."

"The victim was brought out of solitary confinement," the lead agent reminded him.

"Which explains why I'd never seen the dude before," Axel said. "I'd swear on my mother's grave, rest her soul."

"So you didn't know the victim?" the lead agent asked.

"No, sir," Axel replied without hesitation. "Never met him or seen him before."

"Where were you when the victim was brought to the yard?" the lead agent asked.

"I was outside, working out," Axel said. His muscled arms were probably as thick as Ree's thighs. To get arms like those, he had to work out more than a few times a week. "I was on the bench, lifting, when my spotter says, 'Hey, would you look at that?'"

"If you were on the bench, how would you have seen what was happening?" the lead agent asked.

"My spotter," Axel stated, as plain as the nose on his face. "The next thing I heard from him was 'Oh, hell, Ricky is behind him.'"

"Why didn't your spotter come forward?" the lead agent asked.

"He didn't want to end up in a box six feet under for snitching. Inmates take that seriously," Axel informed them. "By the time I sat up, I saw Ricky strangle this guy a couple of feet behind the basket while a game of three-on-three took place. No one stopped, looked, or tried to stop Ricky. Like I said, it's best to mind your own business on the inside. Next thing I know, I'm being hauled in to speak to the warden and I'm being told I'll never make parole." Axel threw up his hands. "There wasn't a thing I could do about it, either."

He issued a sharp sigh.

"They own you when you're inside," he explained. "And if they don't, your crew on the outside does. The people I worked for have long fingers, if you know what I mean. It's not the first time someone died after word spread that they were going to talk to the feds. In fact, it's considered the kiss of death where I come from."

"And who is it you work for on the outside?" the lead agent asked.

Axel leaned forward, then back. He wiped his hands on his pants at the thighs, like he was trying to sop up sweat. Even with his life on the line, it didn't seem to be easy to give up names.

"Who would want the victim dead?" the agent pressed as Marshal Hamlin re-entered the room, and then stood next to the door.

"I give you this information and I get to see my wife and daughter, right?" Axel asked.

Ree figured this wasn't the time to mention the fact his family had considered walking away to stay in a life that wouldn't include him any longer.

"That would be Vadik Gajov." Axel's face went as white as a sheet when he said the name. It was information that could place a bounty on his head.

Ree glanced over at Quint. His hands were fisted, his lips thinned, and every muscle in his face tensed.

"He is the right hand to someone by the name of Dumitru," Axel continued after another sharp sigh. He had to know this was the point of no return. Then again, after they tried to frame him for murder, he had nothing left to lose.

"How do we get to Vadik?" Quint asked, drawing a disapproving sideways glance from the lead agent. The man looked like a real stiff.

This was the information they'd come for. No one should be surprised that Quint was eager to get down to brass tacks.

"I have a contact for you," Axel said quietly. "Her name is Giselle and she'll be friends with your female agent, not you. The operation is run out of Dallas. Giselle can get you invited to a party. She's risking a lot without knowing you're law enforcement, but she'll help you get in when I tell her to. Once there, it's up to you."

"Who is this Giselle and what is her contact information?" the lead agent asked, but Axel looked directly at Ree.

"She'll work with you," he said. "Hand me your phone."

Ree did despite the grunt from the lead agent. Once the contact information was secured in her phone, Quint stood up.

"We've gotten what we came for," he stated.

"I need one more thing," Axel interjected as the lead agent fired off a text. Marshal Hamlin came to the table, moving at a decent clip. From the corner of Ree's eye, she saw Quint's hand twitch and start to make a move for his empty holster.

"Yeah?" Quint asked. "What's that?"

"Protection for Giselle," Axel stated, like he had the power to call the shots. It was an interesting shift, but there was something about the look in his eyes that said this was a nonnegotiable point. Did he want Quint to kiss a ring after this exchange?

"I'm going to need the contact information," the lead agent said, but no one was listening to him anymore.

"I'll tell her to walk away when you reach out to her otherwise," Axel stated. The threat was interesting considering he wasn't exactly in a position to make more demands. Unless he had other information these agencies wanted. Ree understood wanting to protect an asset. She went to great lengths to ensure the people who came forward and trusted her didn't suffer. Crime might pay but the bill was sometimes an informant's life.

"Agent Casey is hardly in charge here," the lead agent protested.

"Why is that so important to you?" Quint asked Axel. "Your family is..."

The reason Axel was so emphatic seemed to dawn on Quint at the same moment it did on Ree. The two had been having an affair.

"Can I ask who she is to you?" Quint asked. They both seemed to realize Axel meant business. He protected the people he loved and he wouldn't want to expose Giselle without giving her a way out of the lifestyle.

"She's family" was all he said. Then he crossed his arms over his chest. He was telling them to make their move.

"I want the contact information," the lead agent said for the third time.

Quint stood there for a long moment like he was contemplating his next move carefully. He'd burned a few bridges in this room and had to know it.

Ree typed out a text to Agent Grappell with the request to secure WITSEC for one more person connected to the case. She tapped the toe of her shoe on the tile flooring while waiting for a response. Two minutes of silence preceded a response. Done.

"Got it," Ree said to Quint.

He looked to Axel. "She'll be offered WITSEC but I can't guarantee that she'll take it."

"She will," Axel said, looking pretty confident. His expression softened when he looked at Quint and said, "Thank you."

"You're welcome," Quint responded. His gaze shifted to the lead agent. "As far as the contact information goes, you'll read it in my report." He turned toward Ree. "Are you ready to go, Agent Sheppard?"

"Thought you'd never ask." Ree was already making her way around the table when Marshal Hamlin blocked their access to the stairs.

"You can call my boss. You can request an investigation into my actions here today. And you can raise hell about me not playing well in the sandbox," Quint growled through clenched teeth. "But if you block my exit, I'll have no problem forcibly removing you."

Axel smirked.

QUINT STOOD IN front of Marshal Hamlin, daring the man to make a move. They'd gotten what they needed to move forward with their investigation. This dog-and-pony show was no longer any use to them. And after the way they'd been treated so far, he wasn't particularly interested in playing nice-nice.

Ree stood beside him, her fingers dancing across the screen of her phone at a record pace. She would most likely be requesting assistance from Bjorn. The concerned wrinkle in her forehead was meant for him. He'd bet money on the fact she wasn't stressed about whether or not he could remove the smug look from Hamlin's face. The wrinkle had appeared the minute she heard the one name that would skyrocket Quint's blood pressure—Dumitru.

Vadik was close to the source. He worked out of Dallas. Giselle could get Quint and Ree inside the man's apartment. Done deal. There was no reason for Quint to hang around. He didn't care about Officer Barns, except to say he had been unlucky. He wouldn't have an out like Axel. Even then, he was going to have to look over his shoulder for the rest of his natural life. Axel knew it. Ree knew it. Quint knew it.

But what choice did the man have? He could go down for a crime he didn't commit and very likely be sentenced to death. Or he could give up information, grab his family and go into Witness Protection for the rest of his life. And it would be a lifelong commitment to their new identities. Tough going considering he had a typical teenager who would have too much access to social media. One slip and she could give away their location. It was clear to anyone paying attention that Axel Ivan loved his family above all else.

If Axel committed himself to whatever new identity he and his family would receive they would have a real shot in life, a second chance to get it right and live on the good side of the law. Quint wished the man luck in his new life.

"Step aside or your boss will get a call from ours." Ree hoisted the text message up to Hamlin's face, stopping within an inch of the screen smacking him right in the nose.

He blinked and took a quick step backward. Quint couldn't wipe the smirk off his face. Ree was a force to be reckoned with and she backed down from no one when she was in the right. Quint almost laughed because she didn't relent when she wasn't right, either. His partner had a stubborn streak a mile long.

Hamlin glanced at the screen before swatting it away and stepping aside. "Be my guest."

"Your hospitality has been much appreciated," Quint said, not bothering to hide his sarcasm. "I'll be sure to request to work with you again real soon on another case."

"Door's tricky," Hamlin said. "Sometimes it can hit

you right in the backside as you exit. I'd be careful if I was you."

The thinly veiled threat made no difference to Quint. Working with other agencies after Tessa's death held no appeal. He needed to figure out a way to keep Bjorn from assigning him to task forces again. This macho, territorial show was for the birds.

Ree led the way out as Quint grabbed the door from her.

"Better watch that one," she quipped as she navigated to the door and then stepped outside into the muggy air. "I hear it has a mind of its own."

Quint chuckled as he walked outside. He felt a whole lot better once he returned his weapon to its holster. Ree's facial muscles relaxed as she did the same before taking the driver's seat.

"Should I take your phone while you drive so I can work out arrangements in Dallas with Grappell?" Quint asked as he struggled with the seat belt. Twisting his body was not a good move if he wanted to stay out of mind-numbing pain.

"I slipped the phone onto my chair and called him with the phone on mute both ways," she stated as she fired up the engine. There was more than a hint of pride in her voice.

"Good idea," he said, duly impressed by his partner. He reached over and touched the back of her hand. The familiar electrical current ran through him at the point of contact.

"I'll point us toward Dallas and somewhere along the

three-to-four-hour drive, Grappell will start hitting my phone with instructions," Ree said. "Are you hungry? Because I could definitely eat."

"We can stop off on the way. It'll give Grappell more time to work out the details," he said. He fished in his pocket for the folded-up piece of paper with the tree on it. "Mind if I use this pen?" He motioned toward the one on the dashboard.

"Go for it," she said. "I didn't even realize it was there."

Quint grabbed the pen as she navigated down the steep incline toward a road that didn't feel like the first drop on a roller coaster. He smoothed the paper out flat on his thigh as he bent over. He made a new branch between Constantin and Dumitru. On the branch, he wrote Vadik's name. He drew a line from Vadik to Dumitru and wrote *right-hand man.* Off to the side in a cloud all on its own, he jotted down the name Giselle. He drew a couple of circles around her name.

"Do you want to stop off at Czech Stop on the way?" Ree asked. This was a gas station, convenience store, and authentic Czech deli rolled into one.

"That can't be a serious question," he quipped.

"I can almost taste a fruit kolache right now," she said with a little mewl of pleasure.

Quint's mind snapped to the last time he'd heard a sound like that from her and an ache welled up inside of him so fast he almost didn't know what to do with it. They were going into a dangerous situation and Quint knew, without a doubt, he would put his life on the line in a heartbeat if it meant bringing justice to Tessa's killer. Dumitru didn't have to be the one to put the bullet in her to be responsible for her death. The jerk didn't deserve to live. He didn't deserve to be the one to have a family and a long life, or any of the things Tessa had been robbed of.

At some point a while later, Ree pulled off the highway. He realized they'd made their exit and he was shocked at how hours could feel like minutes when he was lost in thought. A couple of minutes later, she was parking. Her cell buzzed and she checked the screen before they got out.

"It's our boss," she said, handing over the cell.

"Meet you inside?" he asked.

Ree nodded before exiting the vehicle. She paused as she closed the door like she needed reassurance it was okay to leave him alone on the phone with Bjorn.

"I'll be right in," he said before answering.

"What the hell did you just do, Agent Casey?" Bjorn's voice had the kind of calm that was like looking at the surface of a lake, placid on top while the real danger lurked underneath.

Chapter Thirteen

Ree stood in line, ordered a dozen fruit kolaches and twin cups of coffee, and paid with no sign of Quint. Her own stress levels climbed at what Bjorn might be saying to Quint right now. There was always a possibility he could get pulled from the case—even he had to realize it. The thought of working with a new partner sent the equivalent of a lead ball spiraling through her stomach.

Taking the box of goodies and balancing the coffee cups, she turned around and got a glimpse of Quint in conversation with Bjorn. It wasn't good. Even from here, she could see a vein bulging in his forehead.

With a deep breath, Ree walked outside and to the passenger window. Quint rolled it down immediately and took the box, then the coffees, as she handed them over one at a time. She reclaimed the driver's seat to the sounds of Bjorn's heated dressing-down.

Trying not to focus on what was blasting through her cell, she turned on the engine and navigated back onto the highway. The hum of the road helped drown out Bjorn's screaming. Ree tensed, listening for the moment Bjorn told Quint she was removing him from the case altogether.

Shock of all shocks, Bjorn ended the call saying she needed a full report of what happened and what was said because she didn't appreciate another agency being disrespectful to her agents. Bjorn was the equivalent of an older sibling in that sense. Someone who could dish it out to a younger sibling, but no one else was allowed to.

"That was brutal," she finally said to Quint after he took a couple sips of his coffee.

"I've had worse," he said with a half-smile. He opened the box and held out a kolache, which she managed to eat while driving. "She approved the request for WITSEC, which seemed to matter a whole lot to Axel."

"Think Axel and Giselle were having an affair?" she asked, but already had formed her own opinion on that one.

"Of course, and it had to have started long before he went in," he quickly responded. "I'm not sure if I'm disgusted or respect him."

"Same," she said. The man was cheating on his wife, breaking his marriage vows. But then, he was stepping up and protecting someone who obviously meant a great deal to him. Did he love her? Who knew? The idea he didn't want to throw her under the bus made him seem almost like a decent human being.

In all Ree's years in law enforcement, she'd come to realize everyone had a story. It was rare for someone to come from a good upbringing and turn to crime. She'd seen it but it wasn't the norm. Robbery, jealousy and vengeance were the three main motives behind almost all murders. Committing to a life of crime, a world on the edge of what was considered normal society, was a different ballgame. There, folks typically joined to feel a sense of community or belonging. Crime syndicates replaced traditional families. Some were generational and grew up in neighborhoods controlled by gangs or crime rings. In those cases, going into a life of crime was normalized.

Being part of a family was something Ree understood. There was a need to fit in, belong. Her mother never seemed to catch on to the fact Ree had a need to be her own person. For some reason the girlie gene skipped over her despite her mother's best attempts to force her into wearing hair bows when she was little.

The highway narrowed and road construction was a bear on this stretch, but Ree kept herself from spilling the yummy jelly of her fruit kolache on her blouse. Quint's silence said he realized there would be a reckoning with Bjorn. He seemed to be walking a tightrope. The thought of doing any of this without him caused Ree's chest to squeeze.

"Try not to get yourself kicked off this team, okay?" Ree wasn't sure why she said that out loud, except to say that work wouldn't be the same without Quint. Tracking Dumitru wouldn't be the same without him, either. This was his case and she was along for the ride. The reality of getting one step closer to the ultimate target sat in the silence between them.

"I'll do my best, Ree." There was anguish and resignation in his voice. Another emotion was present too. Regret?

Her cell started buzzing, indicating multiple texts coming in.

"Do you mind?" she asked, motioning toward the noise-maker.

He picked up her phone and started reading. The first text was the address of their new apartment. The second told them their new cover was husband and wife.

"Your alarm system is installed and Shane set it up with the password you requested," Quint finally said.

"That's good news," she stated. "No more surprises. I loved seeing Zoey but it creeped me out that she was able to get inside my home so easily."

"Living out in the country makes it easy to let your guard down," he stated.

"I won't be doing that anymore," she quickly countered. He shot a look like he was asking if she was still talking about the alarm system at her home?

"You're twenty-nine in this scenario," Quint continued. "And a new wardrobe will be waiting for you at the apartment. Agent Grappell said you shouldn't freak out and Bjorn thinks you can pull off the look."

"That's not reassuring," she stated.

Quint seemed amused by all this. "Turns out, we're a partying couple. I supposedly came from Houston and work odd jobs. The story is that I used to come from money but got cut off when I blew through my inheritance at twenty-five years old. Now, I've been 'freelancing,' doing whatever work needs to be done.

I've been a bouncer at a high-end nightclub and had to leave Houston for Dallas to find better quality work."

"You're kind of a loser," Ree teased. "I'm not so certain I want to be in a relationship with someone who doesn't have their act together."

"You happen to be one of those party girls who never seems to have a job but always has money and is always dressed to the nines," he continued, the smirk growing.

"Great. Now I don't even know what I am," she said. There was no doubt she could act the part. That was the basis of undercover work. She could throw on concealer and lipstick, and make herself appear younger. In reality, she wouldn't go back in time for anything. For the first time in her life, she felt like she was finally starting to figure a few things out about herself, outside of who she wanted to be at work.

Ree had been fighting so hard against her mother's image of what she should be that she'd forgotten to look inside herself and decide those things for herself.

"And who are you in this scenario?" she asked.

"I've just been released from prison on a trafficking charge. We're originally from Texas but had been living in Seattle. We're home now for a fresh start," he said.

"I'm guessing Giselle knows people in Seattle," Ree mused.

"It's where she's from," he stated. "And there's something else you should know."

The statement got her attention.

"Giselle has a four-year-old son," Quint informed her.

"Axel?" she asked.

"He's been in jail for the last three years, so I'd put my money on him being the father," Quint stated.

"Certainly explains his insistence on taking care of her," she said. "Wonder why he didn't mention the kid."

"He wasn't ready to tell the other agents in the room," he said.

"They would use it against him," she realized. "Plus, they have direct contact with his wife right now."

"He can't afford for his wife to find out about Giselle," he concluded.

"That would make for serious trouble at home," she agreed. "But I was almost certain Laurie was having an affair when she hesitated to go into WITSEC. At first, I believed she was second-guessing taking her daughter away from everything and everyone she knew and loved, but there was more to it."

"Isn't there always more to the story than meets the eye?" Quint asked.

Ree could say the same about their partnership. Not knowing where they stood, being in limbo, was the worst. At least the case was moving forward now.

QUINT FOCUSED ON the messages as they came in rather than let his mind wander over his last comment. Ree had gotten quiet and he didn't want to get inside his head about what that indicated.

At least he was going to get to do the heavy lifting with Vadik. She would basically play the role of arm candy while he infiltrated. The switch was comforting as they got closer to the evil that had caused Tessa's death. Her baby had been on his mind a great deal lately. Shaking off the anger that came with going down that trail, he refocused on the phone.

"Looks like I'll have a new wardrobe waiting as well as a new car," he stated.

"What will you be driving?" she asked.

"A BMW convertible 4 series in skyscraper-gray metallic," he said. Not bad.

"The appearance of a once-wealthy life of crime. Stinks that you aren't much of a convertible person," she stated.

"When did I ever say that?" he asked.

She laughed and he realized she was teasing.

"Besides, it's part of the cover story. Apparently, after being locked up, I need the open air," he said.

"How long have you been inside?" she asked, figuring they needed to get their stories straight.

"Three years," he continued. "We bottomed out our savings on appeals and finally got a judge to listen. So the story is that I'm in need of work and looking to sell the BMW to keep us going. The apartment where we live belongs to Jenn and Raul, who are out of the country right now."

"What's our last names?" she asked.

"You're Ree Parker-Matthews and I'm Quint Matthews," he stated.

She repeated their names a couple of times. "Got it."

Ree was one of those people who possessed a unique ability to hear something once, repeat it a couple of times and lock it in. Then again, she was one of the sharpest agents he'd ever worked with, no disrespect meant to Tessa's memory.

"What else?" she asked.

"You've been getting by living with your sister and her family for the last three years and couldn't wait to get out of Seattle after my release," he stated.

"A sister?" she balked and that caused him to laugh.

"You really wouldn't know what to do with one of those, would you?" he teased.

"I'll do my best to sell the lie but it's too bad they didn't give me a brother to work with instead," she said. "Brothers, I know."

"Pretend you grew up braiding each other's hair and singing into hairbrushes or something," he quipped.

Ree fake-gagged. "No. Sorry. Can't. My sister will be the marriage-and-family type, while I couldn't stand that noose around my neck. I'm a party girl, remember? I can always say my sister was practically a puritan and we weren't close. That should help."

"We can use the same story about our first date as before," he stated.

"Right. That means we met in Austin," she said.

"I was passing through and stopped off to hear a band," he continued.

"Black Pistol Fire," she immediately stated.

"I like that band, too," he stated.

"They have an interesting bluesy rock-'n'-roll quality, right?" she asked.

"There's something soulful and edgy about their work," he agreed, surprised at the revelation of their music tastes being so similar. He should know these things about Ree instead of how quick she was with a Glock or how capable she was in an altercation. It was strange not to know the basics about someone he'd fallen for. And, yes, Quint could admit to himself their attraction was something far deeper than infatuation.

There was no one else he would want having his back on this investigation and yet her presence made things somewhat problematic. His feelings for her complicated the situation. He was losing his objectivity and some of the burning fire he felt to nail the bastard responsible for Tessa's death was flickering out.

Dumitru belonged behind bars. No one would deny it. Quint needed to be the one to watch the jerk be handcuffed. Better yet, let him be the one who slapped the metal bracelets on the guy.

Tessa and her baby deserved Quint's full attention. She would do no less for him if the situation had been reversed and he was the one six feet under. Recalling the image of Tessa in that hospital bed, lying there lifeless, fueled his anger.

"What happened just now, Quint?" Ree asked, breaking through the fog of his heavy thoughts. "Where did you go?"

"Nowhere," he lied. "It's nothing. I was just trying to memorize the details of our undercover operation. That's all."

Ree sat quietly for a few long moments that seemed to stretch on.

"We were talking about music," he said. "Austin."

She nodded.

"Our first 'date' at the pizza place," he continued.

"Uh-huh," she said absently.

More of that silence sat between them.

"Quint..." she began.

"Yes."

"Don't ever lie to me again," she said simply.

His pulse kicked up a couple of notches. She could read him a little too well and that might backfire in the heat of the moment, when he had to make a critical decision. He could only hope it wouldn't come to that.

Chapter Fourteen

Disappointment sat heavy on Ree's shoulders. When it came to her relationship with Quint, it was always one step forward, two steps back. The push and pull of her attraction to Quint was like fighting against gravity. It was exhausting to say the least. Every attempt to shut it off failed.

Ree wasn't trying hard enough. This man would surely break her heart.

The final minutes of the drive to Dallas were spent with Quint giving her directions from the map feature of her cell phone. The thirty-story high-rise at 350 North Paul Street had all the trappings of a new build.

"What's our floor?" Ree asked, praying it wouldn't be above the tenth floor. She never had been one for heights, preferring to keep her feet on the ground.

"Twenty-seventh," he said, glancing over at her. He did a double take. "What's wrong?"

"Nothing," she lied. "Why?"

"You don't like the setup?" he asked.

"Have I mentioned that I don't love heights?"

"I don't believe you have." He seemed caught off guard by the news.

"I'm not invincible, you know," she stated defensively. "And I'm pretty good at hiding it."

"I'll contact Grappell and see if we can get a lower floor." His gaze shifted back to the screen.

"Don't worry about it. I'll adjust," she stated.

"It's no trouble to ask," he said, but he stopped midtext. They both knew setting up an apartment on such short notice was nothing short of a miracle.

"I'm serious, Quint. I'll figure it out. Besides, we might not even be here long enough for it to matter," she said. It was true. No one knew for certain how quickly a case would go, but the last two seemed to fly by. "We have an in with Vadik by someone inside his circle. It shouldn't be too hard to gather enough evidence to put the man behind bars."

"He's Dumitru's right hand," Quint said. "He won't roll over on him easily. There's a reason he's the guy's second in command."

"I understand that," Ree agreed. "Which is all the more reason we will need to get in and get out. If we give him and his people time, they'll ferret us out. They'll poke around in our backgrounds. The initial meeting and being brought in by someone on the inside will only get us so far."

"Agreed," he said.

"In my experience, and I'm sure the same applies to you, the higher up you go in a crime ring, the faster you want to get in and get out," she stated.

"I'm in this for the long haul, Ree. You already know that. I'll be here for as long as it takes." His grip tightened around her cell phone until his knuckles turned white.

"I am, too, Quint. You're not doing this alone," she reassured him.

He nodded, but she could already see the wheels turning.

"Promise me you won't go off half-cocked, Quint."

The statement seemed to hit home.

"You're my partner, Ree. But if there's a chance to protect you, I'll take it," he said without any hint of apology.

"The best way to protect me is to keep me informed of your every move," she said, and meant it. "No one cares about putting Dumitru behind bars more than you."

Quint nodded.

"Which means we have to keep playing this tight," she said. "We've gotten this far by working together."

"I know," he replied.

Ree was first to exit the vehicle. Quint took his time getting out, looking like he needed a minute to grease the squeaky wheels. She checked the space where the BMW should be parked. Found it. Although she wasn't much of a convertible person, she had to admit it was a beauty.

"The keys are inside the apartment and the door is unlocked. Everything should be waiting in an envelope on the kitchen counter," Quint said, joining her.

He stretched out his arms and yawned. They'd been inside a vehicle for the better part of a day having started early this morning. The saying *feeling like they'd been in a car all day* applied here.

Her own back was sore and she'd long lost feeling in her behind. A walk would do them both some good. There was an ominous feeling sitting heavy on her chest at the thought of crossing the threshold of apartment 2705. One she tried to shake off.

"Do you want to scout the area with me before we head up?" she asked. There'd been a twentysomething guy standing across the street, arms folded, looking like he was trying not to get caught watching their building.

"I need to stretch my legs, too," he said. "Did you see Green Shirt?"

The guy had had on a bright green Polo shirt.

"I was just thinking about him," she admitted. "He could be stalking someone."

"In that loud shirt?" Quint asked. "Maybe."

"Sometimes the best way to blend in is to be loud," she remarked as they started walking.

The block around the apartment teemed with cars. A few of those standup scooters zipped by with mostly young people hanging on to the handlebars. The apartment building sat in the heart of Dallas and was walking distance to quite a few major attractions. The American Airlines Center was nearby, as well as a Dallas favorite, House of Blues. The Dallas Museum of Art wasn't far and neither was Reunion Tower. Katy Trail was easily accessible. There were restaurants along the street. She took note of the location of Highways 75 and I-35. Escape routes were always good to have on hand.

After gaining her bearings, they made the walk back to the building. Dallas wasn't known for its skyscrapers so it would always be easy to find the place. Green Shirt had taken a seat and was playing drums on a set of plastic paint tubs from Home Depot that had been turned upside down. She had to admit, he wasn't bad.

There were two options for heading to the apartment, the main elevators or service elevator. She opted for the latter. Double glass doors led the way into a lobby that resembled another art gallery. This one, as opposed to the Austin house, seemed to let all the light in. Light wood floors. Light walls. Light pictures.

Apartment 2705 was just as impressive.

"You are about to experience six hundred and ninety-four feet of luxury living," Quint said with a wink as he opened the door for her.

"How do you know how many square feet our apartment is?" She must have given quite the look as she walked by because he laughed.

"I looked it up once Grappell gave me the address. Wanted to know what we were getting into," he said, wiggling his eyebrows. The conversation might be lighter now, but the tension between them was still thick. Ree hated it.

She blew out a breath as she walked by, and couldn't help but crack a small smile.

"I, for one, can't wait to see what my new wardrobe looks like," she quipped, figuring there would be more figure-flattering clothes hanging inside. Grappell really had pulled off a miracle getting them this place. It was beautiful, with its smoky, gray velvet couch and coordinating cream-colored fuzzy chairs nestled around a glass end table. The view out the window was amazing even though Ree wouldn't get close enough to truly enjoy it. There was an industrial-looking glass-and-metal dining table with seating for six. It was small and cozy. A man Quint's size would have a time getting comfortable in the midcentury modern forest-green chairs, but she'd seen him make do in her small dinette area. There were two barstools in front of a short counter that separated rooms while still giving an open-concept feel. The kitchen might be on the small side but the cabinets were sleek and the appliances chef-grade. That had always been the irony of urban living. People wanted expensive, high-end kitchens but rarely ever cooked in them. A surprising addition to the kitchen was an under-counter wine fridge. *Nice touch.*

The bedroom was exactly what she expected. One king-size bed in a room that had just enough walking room around it to fit Quint. There were twin nightstands, made of mirrors and steel, and fuzzy throw pillows on the bed. The colors were gray, forest-green and cream. The scheme made it all the way into the master bath.

"At least we can both fit on the bed," she murmured when Quint walked past her. They had to turn sideways for him to pass her in the hallway. Apparently, these luxury apartments had a type, and it wasn't Quint.

"There's a plus," Quint said and there was something low and hungry in his voice that caused all kinds of electrical currents to ripple through her. They were like a livewire at this point, sizzling and curling, causing her stomach to drop.

The air in the room was charged, too, and an ache welled up like a squall inside Ree. The need to touch Quint, to feel his skin against hers, was its own force. They'd made love in Houston and it had been the best of her life. Was there any going back after?

They were stuck somewhere between going all in and taking the plunge to really be together and a dedication to their jobs that reminded them how unprofessional it would be to continue their relationship while on a case.

Ree cleared her throat and walked away, figuring putting some space between them would be a good idea. She located the large yellow envelope on the counter. It wasn't hard to find in a room of gray, green and cream colors. She'd been too distracted by the window earlier to notice it.

She opened the package and emptied the contents onto the counter, where place mats were set up for two. This must be the breakfast bar. At least she had her cell phone and a laptop. There was a cell inside marked with Quint's name on it. Good. He needed a new one after losing his.

Quint joined her a few minutes later.

"The shower in this place is the best part," he said. "Did you check out the closet yet?"

"I didn't have the stomach for it," she admitted with a small smile.

"My new cell?" He picked up the piece of technology after she nodded. He checked the contacts with her standing there, scrolling through fake friends until he stopped at her name, Ree Parker-Matthews. Maybe her new identity could quash her attraction to her partner.

"When this case is over, we need to sit down and have a conversation about us."

"I know," he said with a tone of voice that sounded defeated.

It caused her chest to tighten and a sense of dread to wash over her.

QUINT KNEW REE was right about talking. Nothing in him wanted to sit down with her and break her heart. Hell, he didn't want to break his own heart and the thought of being without her, even for a few minutes, caused an ache like he'd never known.

They were coworkers and terrific partners. He and Tessa used to joke that relationships came and went but a good partnership was forever. Everyone in Quint's life had been temporary. His mother had died too young. His mentor had had a family of his own to keep him busy.

There'd been relationships but none that could measure up to hanging out with his best friend. And now Tessa was gone, too, through no fault of her own. She hadn't wanted to check out at such a young age, especially while pregnant.

A strange thought struck. Did the father of Tessa's baby even know she was gone? The jerk who'd walked away and told her that he didn't want to have anything to do with her or the baby didn't deserve to know what had happened. And yet, a nagging piece of Quint wondered if the guy should know.

The tricky part would be figuring out who he was. Tessa had been tight-lipped. At her funeral, he'd scanned every male face present, searching for some kind of emotion that would give him away. Guilt. Remorse.

If the father of Tessa's baby had been there, Quint hadn't seen him. Another thought struck. Knowing Tessa, she might have not wanted the guy in her or the baby's life. Was it possible she'd made up the part about telling him and him rejecting her?

Quint shook off the thought. There was no way she would lie to him. Right? *Lie* might be a strong word. She'd been known to fudge the truth from time to time. Tessa believed in the gray area, whereas Quint saw things more in black and white. She'd remarked once or twice that he was too literal.

Was he taking liberties now? Had he found the gray area that he wasn't convinced had existed in the past? Everyone had a breaking point, he thought. And he'd always told himself that once he found his, it would be time to get out of law enforcement.

Standing in the breakfast nook, looking at Ree now, he couldn't help but wonder if this was it. Without a doubt, he realized he would do whatever it took to bring down Dumitru. He could chalk it up to the name of justice and probably convince a jury. The problem was facing himself after. How would he do that?

"Are you hungry?" he asked.

"Starving," she said. "The kolaches were amazing but basically too much sugar to hold me for long."

"I could order pizza or walk outside and see what options we have," he said.

She picked up her cell and showed him the screen. "Or you could just Yelp something and save yourself the walk."

"I need to clear my head," he said. "A walk would do me good."

Ree nodded. Then she locked gazes with him.

"After being around Zoey last night, I've decided to get a dog," she stated with the kind of certainty that told him this was a new development to her, too.

"Lots of animals need good homes at the pound," he said, staring at her. Did that mean what he thought? She was considering a change in career. There was something present in her eyes that said this wasn't a good time to ask. So he made a mental note and then tucked his cell inside his jeans pocket.

His mind had been bouncing around from thinking about Tessa, to wondering how far he would go to find and nail Dumitru. Before Ree had entered the picture, avenging Tessa's death had been the only thing he'd thought about. There'd been no clear division between right and wrong. Now, he was starting to question himself.

Before Ree, he hadn't given much thought to his future. Now, all he could think about was being with her when she picked out her damn dog. When did that happen? More of the guilt washed over him when he thought about how much he wanted to kiss those pink lips of hers, too.

This seemed like a good time to head downstairs, get some food and see if Green Shirt was still there.

Chapter Fifteen

Ree didn't care what kind of food she got as long as she ate something soon. She checked the fridge after Quint left. It was bare. Not even a gallon of milk or coffee. She would need to remedy that immediately. She'd never survive without coffee in the morning. There was something about spending a day driving that made her extra tired and her muscles felt like they'd been coiled for the ride up. She stretched out her arms and rolled her shoulders as a text came in.

There were only two things she needed more than air—a shower and a bed, in exactly that order.

The message was from Agent Grappell. Giselle is coming over—get ready.

Ree bit back a curse. She checked to ensure Quint was on the group chat. Thankfully, he was. She made a beeline for the bedroom. The undercover show was about to start and she was dressed way too conservatively to sell her new identity. She also needed to take off her jacket and shoulder holster. Those were dead giveaways.

As she passed a mirror, she also realized there was work to do to her face. There had better be makeup in that bathroom if they wanted her to look younger. Concealer and a bright-colored lipstick at the very least.

The clothes in the closet would be considered scandalous in most circles. Ree slipped on a black minidress that she would not be caught dead in under normal circumstances. The spiked heels with red soles made her tall enough to stand eye-to-eye with Quint. Well, almost.

In the bathroom, there was a basket full of makeup. Thankfully, Grappell seemed to have pulled her records from past assignments because the colors worked with her fiery red hair and green eyes. She let out a yelp when she saw the highlighter brand of makeup she couldn't afford to buy under normal circumstances. Grappell had arranged for her to have the good stuff, too. Too bad she couldn't take any of this home with her when this case was over.

Would it ever be truly over? Not if Dumitru disappeared. Not for Quint.

For his sake, she hoped to be able to break into the inner circle and get in with Vadik. It was a strange thing to wish for because the move would also put Quint's life in danger. There were cases and then there were *cases.* This definitely qualified as the latter. The relentless quality, the torture in Quint's eyes when he thought he was getting closer would never allow him to be at peace until Dumitru was behind bars.

Would it work? She couldn't help but wonder because those things wouldn't bring Tessa back. Her ghost would haunt Quint forever. Ree was beginning to see it so clearly now.

Looking in the mirror, she realized she needed to do something with her hair. There was a curling iron, so she plugged it in. The thing heated up fast. Before she knew it, she'd put a few long, loose curls in her hair. The middle part wasn't something she loved, but it seemed to be the craze, so she went with it.

To finish off the look, she found a glossy lip color that was a deep brown with gold undertones. The name was Consensual. There was a thought, she joked as she opened the round tin before dabbing her finger inside. She tapped the color on her lips before rubbing her lips together to even out the color. *Hey, kid. Not too bad.*

Of course, the "kid" days were long over for her, but she figured this look might convince others she was still in her twenties. This was the rare time having a baby face paid off. Plus, her fair skin had made it impossible to tan in the summer, so she never tried. Now, she was realizing it was more of a gift than a curse because the overly tanned bunch from high school was starting to look a little bit like beef jerky in their pictures on social media. Speaking of which, she sent a text to Grappell reminding him to set up accounts for them under their new identities.

He immediately responded that their social imprint was being worked on. This was the tricky part about a case that came together fast. Creating a believable social-media trail took time and resources.

She made a mental note to bring cookies into the office for Grappell the next time she was in. Having someone like him on the desk made everything else possible. It didn't hurt that she was working on a high-profile case. Even though Dumitru hadn't been the one to pull the trigger, the whole department wanted to see him go down after Tessa's death.

Another text came through that sent her pulse through the roof. Giselle was in the building heading up. Ree slid her holster and Glock in between the mattresses, figuring she'd find a better hiding spot later when she had more time.

Quint texted that he was on his way with pizza and a bottle of wine. This didn't seem like the time to mention they were out of coffee and milk.

She shelved the thought and headed into the kitchen to fill a water glass. A couple of deep breaths on the way and her nerves relaxed a few more notches. An adrenaline spike right before a case went undercover was normal. Deep breaths helped. So did thinking about her family and reminding herself that she would see them again.

Speaking of which, her grandfather wasn't getting any younger. Being on the job made seeing him on the regular a challenge. She missed playing Spicy Uno with him despite his ridiculous rules meant to liven up the game. He looked for all her weaknesses in order to give her more cards, especially the one where no one could talk if a six was played.

By some miracle she wouldn't dare question, Quint made it inside the apartment before Giselle got there.

"How?" she asked but all he did was kiss her. The kiss sent warmth swirling through her and caused all kinds of carnal desires to swim in her head. He pulled back first.

"What was that for?" she asked.

"We're out of practice," he stated. "Plus, I figured us being a couple would be more believable if some of your lipstick rubbed off on me. I've supposedly been in prison for three years and that means I wouldn't be able to keep my hands off you."

"Go change," she said ushering him toward the master and trying to shake off the remnants of that kiss. Her stomach plummeted at his last comment.

As she opened the cabinet to pull out a few plates, a soft knock on the door sounded. Ree walked over, gave herself one last pep talk and then opened the door.

Giselle was the opposite of Laurie. The younger woman had curly blond hair that ran halfway down her back. She was dressed in a crop top and jeans that highlighted a tanned, toned midsection. The woman spent time at the gym. She would regret all that sun later, Ree said to herself.

"Hi," Ree said, ratcheting her voice up several octaves. "Come in."

The twentysomething ducked her shoulders and smiled. "You're friends with Axel?"

"That's right," Ree stated. "But not *friends*, if you know what I mean. We just know each other. In fact, he knows my husband better. I'm Ree Matthews, by the way."

If the last minute was any indication, Ree's cheeks were going to be sore later from smiling so much.

Giselle stepped inside and looked around.

"Nice apartment," she said.

"It belongs to a friend," Ree admitted. "Have you eaten? My husband just brought home pizza and a bottle of wine."

"I could take a slice," Giselle said with an ear-to-ear smile. She was clearly out of her comfort zone and must have cared for Axel a whole lot to trust him this much. Unless…

Did Giselle think she was here for some kind of threesome? The thought was a face slap. Was the young woman for hire? Was that how she knew Axel?

"Make yourself comfortable," Ree said, motioning toward the table. Giselle had the kind of slight frame that would make the dining chairs look roomy. It was difficult to believe a baby had ever been inside that body. She'd certainly bounced back. Although, to be fair, the kid was four years old and that would have made her in her early twenties when she'd had him. "How did you meet Axel?"

Giselle perched on one of the stools before taking off her cross-body bag and hooking it on the back of the chair. She had the kind of annoyingly shiny hair Ree would have killed for in her youth.

"Um, you know, through people," she said, being cautious with information.

At this rate, they wouldn't get anything useful out of her. Then again, she was about to put her life on the line to give them an in with Vadik's people. It was obvious she knew the position she was being put in.

"Where was your husband locked up?" Giselle asked.

"Seattle," Ree said, dodging the question and hoping she could get away with it. They hadn't discussed where he'd been in prison.

QUINT WALKED OUT in time to hear Ree give a pat answer. She gave a quick glance at him, indicating she would appreciate a save. He walked right over to their guest and introduced himself. "You must be Giselle."

"That's right," she said, smiling. Giselle was younger than he expected her to be.

He could admit there was a certain beauty to her, but she was nowhere near on the same scale as Ree. One look at her nearly knocked him over.

"How long have you known Axel?" Giselle asked.

"On and off for five years or so," Quint stated, moving around to the kitchen.

"How about a glass of wine?" Ree asked. "I'm afraid we just got to town and don't have anything else around unless you want water from the tap."

"Wine is good," Giselle stated.

"You got it," Quint said, shooing Ree out of the kitchen after giving her a kiss that left his own lips burning. It might have been for show, but he'd been wanting to do that all day.

Giselle's smile said she approved of the two of them being waited on.

"Axel says I should vouch for you," Giselle admitted.

"I'd appreciate a good word as long as it doesn't put you in a tight spot," Quint said, playing it cool. Sounding too eager was the kiss of death in situations like these.

"No, I'm good. Axel wouldn't ask me to bring you in if he didn't trust you. I trust his judgment," Giselle said. "I just thought we should get to know a little more about each other before we head to the party tonight."

"Tonight?" Quint asked before he could reel the question back in.

"We have time for you to eat your pizza," she said quickly. "Can't have anyone showing up on an empty stomach."

Quint opened the wine and poured three glasses, figuring Ree needed one after hearing the news they would be up later tonight than planned. It was good, though. There was no time like the present and he'd waited long enough for a break. Some cases shot right out of the gate while others lagged, taking time. Now that there was action, this one seemed ready for the express train.

He set down the glasses on the counter and then plated the slices. After passing out the plates, he picked up his own and ate. Talking slowed, which meant everyone was hungry.

Giselle pulled her cell out of her purse after she'd polished off the last bite. She set it down on the counter. "I should probably get your contact info while I'm thinking about it."

"Oh, good. Right," Ree stated.

"I meant Quint's," Giselle clarified. There was something worldly about her, like she was someone who knew the ropes and partied most nights. It wasn't the motherly image he expected from Axel's mistress. Then again, his wife was with their daughter. The three of them were a "traditional" family, whereas Giselle was something on the side. Quint wondered if there were others like her and her son for Axel.

Speaking of which, the photo on her screensaver was of a little dark-haired boy who resembled his father.

"This must be your son," Ree stated. "Axel talked about him."

"He did?" Giselle sounded surprised and a little bit proud.

"Yes, of course," Ree said. "Your son is adorable."

"He stays with my sister," Giselle said, her shoulders slumping forward, looking deflated. "But Axel always makes sure Axel Junior has everything he needs."

"I'm sure he does," Quint said. "I know how proud he is of his boy."

The comment seemed to win favor with Giselle, who brought up her pictures and scrolled through a few.

"He hasn't been able to spend much time with his daddy, but they're two peas in a pod," she said, showing Axel holding his son as an infant. She looked to Ree. "Do you have kids?"

"Me? No," she said quickly. "Not with Quint locked

up for the past few years. I had a scare when he first went in, but it turned out to be a false positive."

"Oh, I'm sorry," Giselle said sympathetically. She reached over and touched Ree's hand. "That must have been hard."

"I think it turned out for the best," Ree said. "I was already living with my sister in Seattle. I would have wanted Quint to see our kid take its first steps and do all that stuff kids do."

Giselle took a long pull of wine.

"Axel has missed out on a lot while locked up. Laurie gets all the visitation days, so I haven't been able to see him since he went in," Giselle admitted.

"That must be hard," Ree said with as much sympathy as it looked like she could muster.

"It's been okay," she said, sitting up a little straighter. "He said things will be different now that he's being released. He said Axel Junior and me will be together and that I shouldn't worry."

Quint nodded, thinking the faster he got in and got evidence, the better, now that Axel had turned state's witness. Vadik would surely come after Giselle the minute word got out and there was no way to know when that would happen.

The other question looming was whether or not these arrests would spook Dumitru into heading back overseas until everything cooled. The only thing they had working in their favor was the man's ego. If he believed himself to be untouchable, his arrogance could be his downfall.

This close, Quint could almost taste the victory. *A bad sign*, he thought. Their recent successes might be making him feel foolproof. The old saying *pride comes before the fall* came to mind.

"I'll have to bring Ree into the party first and then check to see if it's okay if her husband can come," Giselle stated. "It's a lot easier to bring a chick into Vadik's apartment than a dude."

Quint's blood pressure shot up a few notches but he managed a calm smile.

"You really can't be too careful these days," Quint said, knowing full well if he seemed too interested he might tip her off. No matter how much she loved Axel, she might not go along with the plan if she knew she was working an undercover sting operation. Her life was on the line and that wasn't something Quint took lightly. Knowing she was a single mother hit home. Despite her partying ways, there was something in her tone when she spoke about Axel and their son that convinced Quint she would much rather be part of a family than stay in this life.

Choices were a strange thing. When Quint was younger and in near-constant trouble, he'd told himself that he didn't have a choice. Everyone around him walked on the wrong side of the law, save for his mother, whom he barely saw. And then Officer Jazzy had come along at just the right time in Quint's life. The school liaison officer showed an interest in Quint's life and helped him realize circumstances didn't determine a life, choices did.

The lesson hadn't come easy or been developed overnight, but once Quint realized the power he had over his own choices, rather than allowing his environment to take the wheel, he knew he was ready to make changes. He designed his life and his career from there. He had everything he thought he'd ever wanted. *Except the right person to share it with*, the annoying voice in the back of his mind reminded him. Now, the thought of putting her at risk for his revenge sat heavy on his chest.

Chapter Sixteen

Ree could already get a read on Giselle. Her son was important to her even though he didn't live with her. Kids in general seemed important, too. Ree had made a couple of slips when talking about kids. Giselle's son not living with her seemed like a big deal. The fact that Axel said they would be reunited soon sent up a few alarms. He'd negotiated for WITSEC for his mistress and their love child. Clearly, no one had told her about that part of the bargain. Was that a total surprise? Not as much as it should be.

Quint entered his cell-phone number into Giselle's contacts. The act shouldn't bother Ree and yet seeing him giving out his number to someone so young and pretty caused a surprising reaction. She needed to get over it and fast, now that the case was growing legs.

"What time is the party?" Ree asked.

"It starts at seven thirty." Giselle checked the time on her phone. "Or maybe I should say *started*."

The time was quarter to eight. Ree stifled a yawn, figuring she could fall asleep right there on the stool if no one would notice. Since she couldn't get away with that, she took a sip of wine and gave herself a mental headshake. Having food in her stomach only made her more tired. Coffee would wake her up better than wine.

"We should probably get going. Vadik likes chicks there early." Giselle tucked her phone inside her purse and stood up.

"How far is his place from here?" Ree asked.

"It's only two blocks," Giselle stated. "We should be able to walk it fine."

"If it comes up, I have a BMW I'm thinking about selling," Quint stated.

"You love that car, hon," Ree interjected, playing the sympathetic wife.

"I love you more and we need the money." He walked over and hauled her against his chest, reaching around to squeeze her bottom. The familiarity between them helped them sell the lie they were together and Giselle wouldn't expect to be around the kind of guy who held back from taking what he wanted.

The move seemed to work. Giselle blushed before excusing herself and waiting at the door. It also bought a few seconds of privacy.

"I'll be close if you need me," Quint whispered in her ear.

Ree didn't have to push up to her tiptoes in these heels. She planted a kiss on Quint that made her own bones melt. She'd missed this between them. Being a married couple while undercover felt like the most natural thing once they got over the initial hump of getting to know each other. Working side by side without being in constant physical contact since their last case ended seemed strange to her now.

After another steamy kiss, Ree headed toward the front door. Giselle's hand was on the knob and she was absently scrolling on her cell phone when Ree walked over. The clicking of her heels on the tile flooring gave Giselle a heads-up.

"Let's go," Ree said to a smiling Giselle.

"Fair warning," Giselle stated. "Vadik has a thing for redheads."

"Good to know," Ree said. "I'm taken, by the way."

"Just make sure you know that," Giselle stated, heading toward the elevator bank. "Vadik can be convincing when he really wants to be and I've seen more than a few couples break up over him."

"I'm solid with Quint," Ree stated. "What about you?"

"Oh, I'm not his type and I'm with one of his people," she said. "He and Axel go way back."

Ree wondered how far because she was also worried Vadik was the one who'd sent the Acura driver to do away with Laurie and Ariana. Although, someone might have been getting to them in order to hold them over Axel's head. It was impossible to know if they were meant to be kidnapped or murdered at this point.

Ree made a mental note to read the report tonight. It was possible something had been found inside the Acura that might clue them in. Her nerves tingled at the thought of going into Vadik's apartment so soon. A whole lot had happened in the last few days. Introducing a new person right now was risky.

Were they moving too fast?

"Vadik can be a little handsy at first. If you get to meet him tonight, that is," Giselle said. "I'm sure you know how to handle dudes like him."

"Sure can," Ree said, thinking she'd like to drop him to the mat if he tried anything with her. Playing a helpless party girl made her want to vomit. It was so the opposite of Ree's natural personality. She tucked in all her tomboy tendencies for the time being. *Unnatural*, she thought.

Thankfully, these cases didn't last forever. She would die in these heels and the skirt was already riding up, giving all the people on the street a bird's-eye view of her long legs. She could only hope nothing was hanging out. Resisting the urge to reach around to her backside and check, she asked, "How about you? How did you meet Axel?"

"At one of Vadik's parties," Giselle said as a blush overtook her cheeks. "I'm originally from Mexia. Do you know where that is?"

"I sure do." Ree knew exactly where it was—about an hour and twenty minutes south of Dallas and east of Waco. There was no viable public transportation between Dallas and Mexia except by car. "Did you like living in a small town?"

"No. I hated it. There was never anything to do and my childhood was boring," Giselle stated. "I worked at the DQ in high school before dropping out."

"What brought you to Dallas?" Ree asked.

"Are you kidding? I would have been willing to move anywhere else to get away from Mexia," Giselle said.

Ree didn't agree. She loved the quiet of a small town. The peacefulness and the way neighbors still knew each other. She loved being part of a community. Although, to be fair, with her work schedule she hadn't been to a town fair or tree-lighting ceremony since she could remember. College?

"But I had a friend moving here who said we could work as waitresses in a strip club on Harry Hines," Giselle stated. "My friend met one of his guys and soon after we were invited to one of these parties. That's how I met Axel."

What a family man, Ree thought wryly.

"We hit it off right away and he convinced Vadik to hire me to work his parties as a cocktail waitress so we could spend more time together," she said. Again, she blushed. It was clear the woman had deep feelings for Axel.

"What a sweetie," Ree said, forcing the sarcasm out of her tone.

"I know. Right?" Giselle agreed, turning a darker shade of crimson.

They turned the corner at the end of two blocks. "This is it. This is Vadik's building."

The all-glass structure looked like something out of a futuristic movie.

"He's on thirty-three. The penthouse," Giselle said.

"When I'm in there—" she pointed toward the sky "—I go by Gigi."

"Got it," Ree said, her body involuntarily shivering at the thought of being that high in the air. "I'm just Ree no matter where I am." It was true. She always used her real first name when she was undercover. It reduced her chances of making a mistake and giving out the wrong name straight out of the gate. Nothing was perfect, though. It also made it easier to keep going with her real last name.

"Cool," Giselle said as they entered the building. The outside might look futuristic, but the inside was a cool chic that resembled a high-end hotel. There was a concierge waiting behind an all-glass counter. He immediately started to come around to greet them until his gaze landed on Giselle. He simply nodded and returned to his spot, looking down like he'd just witnessed a mob crime and knew better than to stare.

The Italian marbled tile had probably been flown over piece by piece. Ree had thought her building was nice until she stepped inside this one. The sound of their heels clicking on the flooring echoed across a massive lobby. There was an abundance of seating and no one taking advantage of it. There was also a table with a rather large glass water server on the back wall with enough small clear cups to hydrate a small army.

The glass elevators weren't Ree's favorite. She sucked in a breath and grabbed on to Giselle's arm.

"They're freaky, right?" Giselle stated. She had the

glamour of a party girl but there was still a hint of her small-town accent. “These elevators, I mean.”

“I’m not a fan of heights,” Ree admitted, trying not to dig her nails into Giselle’s flesh. “Sorry.”

“Don’t be,” Giselle said. “Whatever helps get you through is all right by me.”

As the elevator dinged, indicating their arrival on the penthouse floor, Giselle grabbed a pill bottle out of her purse. “Do you want one?”

They stepped out of the elevator and the doors immediately closed behind them.

“What is that?” Ree asked. She didn’t know what she was being offered based on the bottle’s label. People went to great lengths to camouflage their drugs in the simplest of containers.

“It’s a muscle relaxer,” Giselle stated. “It’s pretty lightweight so you’ll still be able to drink at the party. Takes the edge off, if you know what I mean.”

“The last time I took one of those, I almost passed out after two glasses of wine,” Ree lied.

“Better not do that.” Giselle closed her hand around the pair of white pills. She dry-swallowed them. “The dudes who come through can pretty much get away with anything they want. They walk past and want to pat you on the tail, and they get to as long as you’re not claimed by somebody else. Even then, if he’s not in the room some dudes might take advantage. We aren’t allowed to complain, get sloppy, or hang all over someone who isn’t in to it.”

All Ree could think was how the Me Too movement seemed to have slipped past these jerks.

"So it's basically like all the parties I've been to in the past but in a better building," Ree quipped, trying to build some camaraderie.

Giselle rolled her eyes, blew out a breath and smiled. "Seriously. Crappy, right?"

"I've been to worse places with a whole lot worse people," Ree stated. In all honestly, she had, too.

"Same," Giselle said with another eye roll. She pulled a key out of her purse. "Only VIPs get these. We'll walk in and head straight to the kitchen. Just follow me and you'll be fine."

Ree touched Giselle's arm.

"Do I look okay?" She shouldn't be nervous but she couldn't help it and it was easy enough to play it off as party jitters.

"You? You're amazing," Giselle said with a hint of admiration. "Don't even worry about it. Everyone will love you."

"I hope you're right," she said. She always got a burst of adrenaline and was hit with doubts right before walking into a risky situation. Normally, it energized her and kept her sharp. Fear kept her alert.

This time, a sense of dread filled her, along with the very real thought she might not walk out of here again. She had no place to put a backup weapon and no way to communicate with Quint other than a cell phone.

But this was her job and she'd complete this mission no matter the cost.

Chapter Seventeen

Giselle unlocked the door, tucked the key back inside a small pocket in her purse and walked in like she belonged. Ree followed suit, taking in the massive corner room with two walls of windows. The views here were even more incredible than at her place. There was land as far as the eye could see. The room was shaped like a square and she had to take two steps down to enter the space. Twin couches faced each other and there was enough seating around both for a dozen or more people to gather. To the right of the room was a glass bar complete with a bartender. There was a hallway she assumed led to the kitchen, but it was tucked away off to one side. Another hallway on the opposite side must have led to bedrooms.

The second that her and Giselle stepped inside, they were patted down by two men in suits who looked like they should be in a *Godfather* movie and not here in Dallas. One requested she open her purse. She did, so he could look inside. He felt around for a secret lining.

Vadik was thorough. She would give him that. And had a decent decorator.

Everything in the space was black, white and gray. Modern was the best way to describe it and nothing looked especially comfortable, like a sofa she could sink into and watch a movie. But then, she highly doubted movie premieres were the purpose of this room. In fact, she didn't see a screen anywhere.

Ree followed Giselle into the kitchen as a few heads turned toward them. There was a sea of average-looking men who were dressed nicely. The women in the room were the real showstoppers. Not a surprise given the fact that Vadik seemed like a class-A chauvinist based on what Giselle had just said in the hall.

Arresting a jerk like that always gave Ree an extra boost of pride. It felt good to take another womanizer off the street before he could pass on his ideology to the next generation of young men. Doing so was infinitely trickier from behind bars.

In the kitchen, more folks stood around talking, much the same as in the living room. There were a few couples and then others who weren't so clearly matched up standing around. Another make-Ree-puke fact was the ratio of men to women. To say the scales were tipped to more women was an understatement. The number of females didn't double the number of males, but it came close.

"Nice night, Gigi," one of the men Ree recognized from the Wanted database said to Giselle. He walked up and slung his arm around her like she was his possession. His name was Sylvester Keeting, but his nickname was Sly as an homage to the actor in the Rocky Balboa movies.

"Hey, Sly," Giselle, calm as anyone could be, remarked. It was clear to Ree the woman loved Axel, so this had to feel slimy to her. "How's Angie?"

"Good. Home with the kids," he said. Based on the slurring of his words, he was already a little bit drunk.

"Tell her I'm real sorry to hear about her mother," Giselle said, strategically shrugging out of Sly's grip as she made a move for the cheese platter.

"How have you been?" Sly continued, not bothered by the attempt to duck out of his grip. He simply dropped his hand and squeezed her bottom.

"Real good lately," she said, keeping her voice even. To a drunk, she would seem compliant. To anyone halfway sober, they would feel the chill rolling off her in palpable waves. "Have you seen him?"

Sly took a step to the side. He seemed to sober up when she mentioned *him.* She could only mean one person—Vadik.

"Last I heard, he was on the patio with Gorge," Sly said, his tone suddenly far more serious than it had been. Good to know all she had to do was mention *him* and the men seemed to stand up a little straighter. They might be given a free pass to sexually harass women but there seemed to be lines even they wouldn't cross.

"Do you know what they were talking about?" she asked.

"None of my business," Sly said. He was five feet

ten inches. Slicked-black hair and a large nose made him resemble the Italian from the movie, except that was where the similarities ended. Rocky's character might be a thug, but he stood up for the little guy. He collected debts for guys like Vadik because he didn't want to starve, not because he was a jerk who enjoyed torturing others. Sly was wanted for human trafficking. Not exactly a stand-up guy. He turned his attention on Ree. "Who is the redhead over here?"

"I'm Ree," she said, smiling as she twirled a strand of hair in her finger to flirt a little bit. Did it make her stomach turn? Yes. It was necessary to do her job.

She made another mental note to check out Sly's rap sheet later while she read the report on the Acura driver. This was one of those times she wished she'd been able to fix some kind of communication device on herself so she could send information back to Quint more easily. Excusing herself to go to the bathroom would draw attention.

Strangely, no female was on her phone, unlike pretty much everywhere Ree went outside of this apartment. It was odd how dependent everyone had become on those devices that were practically glued to their hands.

The guys did whatever they pleased. One stood in the corner of the room looking out a window while on his cell. He spoke quietly, so she couldn't pick up what he was saying. There was a low hum of conversation along with a Frank Sinatra song playing in the background.

Vadik must consider himself a renaissance man. Interesting, she thought as Sly sidled over next to her. He tucked an errant strand of hair behind her ear and, once again, her stomach turned.

"She hasn't met *him* yet," Giselle warned.

Those words were all that was required for Sly to bring his hand back, as though he'd just touched a hot stove. There must be an approval required for interaction. She would thank Vadik later, oncc hc was wearing handcuffs.

Sly worked his way around the granite island, nibbling and watching as Giselle poured a couple of glasses of wine then handed one over. She clinked glasses with Ree and said, "Bottom's up."

Ree took a long pull off the wine. "There's a bar in the other room."

"It's for the men. Vadik doesn't think it's ladylike for a chick to stand at the bar," Giselle explained. "He keeps wine back here for us."

"Let me guess, he doesn't think it's proper for a woman to drink anything else," Ree mused.

Giselle nodded.

The double standard would normally frustrate Ree to no end. She could throw back a shot as well as any one of her brothers despite not being a big drinker. Her brothers had always joked it was their Irish heritage that gave her such a high tolerance. She'd thank her DNA later.

"Give me a minute, will you?" Giselle asked. For reasons Ree couldn't explain, the thought distressed her. The ominous feeling she'd had at the door returned and she couldn't for the life of her figure out why.

"Sure. Go ahead." Ree tried not to notice the grin on Sly's face at having her alone in the kitchen.

Cell Phone Guy ended his call about the time Giselle made her exit. She was most likely going to speak to Vadik about Ree being here and hopefully lay the groundwork for Quint to work for the organization like Axel did, thereby infiltrating the organization and ultimately leading him to Dumitru. She took note of the fact Axel had asked them to keep quiet about the WITSEC part of the deal. He didn't want her to be told about it until arrests were made. The decision hinted toward him possibly not trusting her enough to keep the secret.

"What's your name?" Cell Phone Guy asked.

"Ree," she responded. "What's yours?"

"Cedric," he said as he walked over. "What happened to Gigi?"

"She went to talk to Vadik about me, I guess," Ree admitted.

"Must be your first time here then," Cedric said as Sly made his exit. There were others in the room. A couple standing by the fridge who should probably be in one of the bedrooms instead of out in the open. Their hands were all over each other. A mistress? This seemed to be the place.

On her way in, Ree hadn't seen a whole lot of women who looked like they'd had kids. Then again, Giselle was tiny. No evidence of carrying Axel's baby on her slight frame. Ree wasn't sure what she thought a mother looked like, but Giselle didn't match that description, either. She had her own sister-in-law to compare everyone to. Evelyn was the ultimate in home and heart. She baked from scratch and cooked most every day. Evelyn loved being pregnant and said she'd never felt better than when she was carrying a baby. More evidence that Ree wasn't cut out for that kind of life.

Except that since meeting Quint she could see herself married with kids. But not so she could stay home and bake every day. She would be more like the reheat in the microwave kind of mom.

Ree shook off the thought. The notion she was considering what kind of parent she would be was a foreign one. It should make her uncomfortable but felt like the most natural thing with a partner like Quint.

Being honest with herself, she could admit he was special to her.

Giselle reappeared and walked straight over to Ree, taking her by the hand and making eyes at her that said *follow my lead.* Ree didn't seem to have a choice as Giselle did an immediate about-face, walking them in the direction from where she'd come a few seconds ago. She didn't stop until they reached the open double doors that led out to an expansive balcony. The three-quarters wall keeping her from falling down thirty-three stories was made of a concrete-and-stone mix.

Stepping outside, this was the moment Ree prayed the engineer who'd built this building knew what he was doing and that she wouldn't plummet to her death. There were quite a few people out here already and she had no idea if there was a weight tipping point that would bring the structure crashing down with her and everyone else along with it.

Taking a deep breath meant to fortify herself, she kept walking, careful not to look to her left. Instead, she focused her gaze on the concrete flooring. When Giselle stopped, Ree looked up.

The man standing in front of them had dark hair and slate-gray eyes. He stood with his arms folded, like he was inspecting her, deciding if she made the cut. There was something about his scrutiny that made her feel like she wanted to put on a sweater.

Then, he smiled and gave a slight nod. Giselle seemed to breathe a sigh of relief before giving him Ree's hand. The move only contributed to the awkwardness of the meeting.

"This is Ree," she said.

He gave another show of white, crooked teeth. In the animal kingdom, this would be reason for worry. Humans might view the act differently but it had the effect on Ree of the wildlife version.

Vadik was five-nine to five-ten, no more or less, which was average for elsewhere but not in Texas. Here, he was on the short side.

"Ree's husband is in the market to sell his BMW," Giselle stated as Vadik took his time perusing Ree.

She wanted to go home and take a shower after he was finished. He seemed pleased with her appearance and this seemed like a good time to remind herself she'd passed muster. This would give her access to the inner circle and she would remember the look on his face when she busted him, which would hopefully be soon. There was no telling how quickly word about Axel would get out and his mistress would go down right along with him. Now that Ree thought about it, she wondered why that hadn't happened already. Speed Runner had been sent to pick up the wife and teen, or murder them. The jury was still out since Ree hadn't had a chance to read Grappell's report—a report that should be uploaded by now.

"I haven't seen you before. Where did you come from?" Vadik finally said in a thick Eastern European accent.

"I've been living in Seattle with my sister while my husband was locked up," Ree said, disengaging her hand from Vadik's the second she thought she could get away with it.

A mix of emotions passed behind his eyes in a flicker. Surprise. Jealousy. Desire. Had she just made herself a challenge in his eyes? A chauvinist like him would see her refusal of an advance in that light.

"Where is he now?" Vadik glanced around.

"At home. We just moved a couple of blocks away," Ree stated.

"Why is he selling his car?" Vadik asked.

Ree could slip in the poor-us line and tell him they needed the money. Except it was too obvious and, in her opinion, too pushy coming from her. Instead, she shrugged. "You know men and their cars. They love them one day and the next they want something new."

She fluttered her eyelashes at him, then added, "Not unlike the relationship they have with their women."

"I can't imagine a man ever getting tired of you," Vadik said before turning his attention toward a man to his left.

Realizing she'd been excused, she walked away. No, *walked* wasn't nearly close enough to what she did. It was more like a saunter that was meant to draw attention to her backside and the gentle sway of her hips.

After standing at the kitchen island and slowly sipping her wine for half an hour while fighting off the exhaustion of the day, someone came up behind her and took her by the arm. She turned in time to meet Vadik at eye level.

"If your husband is looking for work, I might have something for him," Vadik said.

"I can ask if he'd be interested," she said, trying her best to act nonchalant.

"He is," the man responded with a threatening look.

Ree stood up a little straighter. "I'll text him right now to come meet you."

Vadik nodded, and then retreated to the balcony along with his entourage of four men in suits. Bodyguards? Then a twentysomething woman done up in a miniskirt and a shirt that was missing the bottom half appeared. Abs on full display, the woman could barely walk on the heels that were more like stilts.

The second she got close to Vadik, he snaked his arm around her waist and pulled her against his body without missing a beat in his conversation. As Ree texted the okay to Quint, the man on the patio ignored the woman plastered against him. The term *arm candy* came to mind. Again, Ree's body involuntarily shivered at the thought of being treated like an afterthought. She literally would rather be single for the rest of her life than settle. Besides, she'd done all right for herself alone.

She'd worked, saved and bought a home that she loved. She had a career and, more importantly, a reason to get out of bed every morning. She had an exciting job even if the shine was starting to wear off the dangerous side. And she planned to get a puppy, especially after spending time with Zoey's. Ree was smart. She could figure out how to manage her job and care for a dog. She had family to count on. One of her brothers would watch Fido—or whatever its name was—if she asked.

And so what if she was suddenly starting to notice she hadn't been in a long-term relationship for far too many years? It wasn't like meeting new people had been high on her priority list lately.

Another hand on her arm caused her to suck in a sharp breath.

"Sorry," Giselle said. She smiled from ear to ear. "Looks like your husband is in."

Ree nodded and returned the smile but with less enthusiasm. Quint was in. Now, the real danger began.

Chapter Eighteen

Quint waited for twenty minutes before leaving the apartment and then took his time walking the couple of blocks to Vadik's building, suppressing the urge to bolt right over after receiving the text from Ree. Eagerness reeked of desperation.

He texted Ree the minute the elevator doors closed. She and Giselle met him at the top.

Quint brought Ree into an intimate embrace before kissing her. He turned his attention toward Giselle and thanked her for mentioning him to Vadik.

"I don't think he's interested in the car," Giselle said on a sigh.

"Work is good," he quickly stated.

She nodded before leading them inside the apartment, where Quint was immediately searched. Once he was given the green light, Giselle walked him to the balcony, took Ree's hand from his and excused them both.

Vadik's gray eyes met Quint's. He could tell a whole lot about a person by looking into their eyes. There was a cruelty in his that spoke of pure evil. Vadik gave a slight nod and two men who'd been standing huddled together near the balcony entrance came toward Quint.

"Come with us," one of the guys said.

Quint was walked out a side door by the kitchen and onto the service elevator, where a third man stood holding open the door. He had on a suit and black, shiny shocs Quint would expect to see worn with a tuxedo.

No one asked if he wanted to go, but if he didn't, it was clear he would be escorted out forcefully. Not exactly a good sign.

"I'm Quint," he said to Shiny Shoes, who popped up his chin in response.

"Chef," he said and Quint probably didn't want to know where the nickname originated from. "Over there is Keith and next to him is Samuel."

The color of the evening seemed to be black. Chef had on a black mock turtleneck and dark slacks. Keith wore black slacks with a black-and-white checkered shirt that looked to be a size too small. His arms bulged, as though his muscles might break through the material restraining them. Then there was Samuel. He had on silvery gray slacks with a black cotton button-down shirt. Keith had a thick neck and looked like someone who'd just walked off a rugby pitch, whereas Samuel had more of a lean, runner's build. He looked wiry, like the kind of guy who could surprise a person with his strength. Then, there was Chef. Black on him did little to hide his big stomach. It was large and round, and what most people would refer to as a beer belly, or beer baby depending.

Quint himself had on an all-black ensemble. His black button-down shirt was shinier than the others'. His slacks were off-the-rack, while theirs had a tailored quality. Maybe they shared the same guy, or Vadik liked the people surrounding him to look a certain way. It was the illusion of class, since any one of the men upstairs, or in this elevator, would probably rip off a person's head at Vadik's command.

"Where are we headed, fellas?" Quint asked as an uneasy feeling settled over him. Ree was upstairs and there was no way to get a message to her.

"Phone. Wallet. Keys." Chef held out his hands, beggar-style.

Quint emptied his pockets. While Ree was at the party, he'd secured their home just in case. If these guys took him back to his own apartment to search it, they would be covered. Being caught off guard earlier had clearly rattled Ree. She'd pulled it together and looked the part by the time he'd returned with the pizza, but she'd had very little in the way of advance notice.

The foursome left the service elevator and walked into an alley. Keith picked up a rock and tossed it at the light over the door, shattering it. They were plunged into darkness.

"I heard you got picked up by Dallas PD a couple of days ago," Chef said. "What the hell were you doing in North Dallas?"

"Helping out a friend," Quint said. There would be a record of his arrest and he hadn't played the ATF agent card on purpose. He was undercover and didn't want to blow it.

"Who do you really work for?" Chef said.

A light came on. One of those flashlight apps on a cell phone. Quint squinted against the near-blinding light.

"No one," he said. Hc barely got the words out when the first punch landed. He bent forward and dropped to his knees. He muttered a string of curses as pain ripped through him.

"You don't want to tell us?" Chef said.

Another blow came. This time, striking his shoulder. Quint grunted and blew out a couple of sharp breaths in succession, trying to slow the agony.

"I can't," he stated. "I went freelance. Got a message to pick up a chick and her teenage daughter. Apparently, I wasn't the only one. Cops came and I ended up getting arrested along with another guy. That's all I know."

"How'd you pick up the assignment?" Chef pressed, agitation in his voice.

"A blind call on the internet," Quint confessed right before the toe of a hard shoe drilled into his thigh.

For a split second, he thought about fighting back. Everything inside him wanted to take these men out. Permanently. A second kick was the heel of a shoe to his kidneys. That one dropped him onto the pavement. Quint curled in a ball to protect his vital organs as Keith and Samuel gave him their best. The blows were felt much more on top of his previous injury. His vision blurred and the room started to spin from pain.

"Stop," Chef finally said.

Now, everything hurt. There wasn't a part of his body that wasn't screaming in pain.

A few extra punches came before Chef seemed to put his body in between Keith and Samuel. No doubt about it, these were Vadik's henchmen.

"You need a hand up?" Chef asked.

"No. I got it," Quint immediately said. His pride wouldn't allow for it unless it was absolutely necessary for the case. It wasn't, and there was no way in hell he was taking a hand from one of these bastards. Slowly, he managed to sit up. His head was spinning, and for a second, he thought he might black out.

"Go up," Chef ordered his cohorts in a surprise move.

Keith and Samuel didn't say a whole lot. They seemed to speak with their fists and the message was loud and clear—don't betray Vadik. They were letting Quint know his life depended on it.

The light disappeared and then a few seconds later, the door opened and closed. One of the guys put a rock in the way, keeping the door cracked for Chef.

"You need something?" Chef asked.

Quint grunted.

"I got into a scuffle and then ended up stabbed before I got arrested," Quint said in between grunts. "But I'm fine."

"Yeah, you sound like it," Chef said with a chuckle. He seemed to respect Quint's honesty. "The boss likes for people to know what they're getting into before he gives them a job. Not a lot of people pass the test, if you know what I mean."

"Did I?" Quint could already feel himself bleeding through his shirt. Dammit.

"I think so," Chef said. "Now, I'll give you a hand up if you need one but I gotta get back upstairs."

"Nope. I said I got this and I do." With great effort, Quint got to his feet. He took two steps and had to grab on to the wall to stay upright. "If I wasn't already banged up, those two wouldn't have been able to do this much damage."

Chef held the door open and smiled. "For some reason, I believe you."

GISELLE CAUGHT REE'S attention and glared at her. She made a face to go along with it.

Ree twisted her hands together and forced herself to stop pacing in the kitchen. She pressed flat palms against the cool granite. She took in a couple of slow breaths before picking up her wineglass and taking another pull.

The back door opened and two of the men who'd escorted Quint outside walked in. They made a beeline for the balcony, where Vadik was in lip-lock with Disco Skirt. He had her up against the railing, both hands to either side of her, trapping her. What was he afraid of? She couldn't exactly run away unless she jumped.

Ree's pulse kicked up a few notches when she saw one of the guys tug at the other one's sleeve. He nodded back to the kitchen, where they went to the sink and washed blood off their hands. One shook out his hand like it still burned from punching someone. Where was Quint?

Giselle started toward Ree when the back door opened again. This time, a big guy walked inside with Quint following. He looked to be in bad shape. His shirt was blood-soaked and there was no sign of him bruising on his knuckles.

He walked straight over to Ree and kissed her. The move, she noticed, also allowed him to lean on her without looking like he was about to collapse. He was showing strength but she could see that he was about to drop.

"We have to go, Gigi," she said to Giselle. "We'll come back another time."

"Let me walk you out," Giselle said.

"No, thanks," Ree countered. "We know the way to the door. We'll be fine."

"Call me later," Giselle said, more than a hint of concern in her voice.

"I will," Ree stated. She let Quint throw a possessive arm around her as they walked to the door and out to the elevator. The minute the doors closed, he slumped onto the railing. "What happened to you?"

"They asked about the arrest," he groaned.

"They must have someone watching out at Dallas PD," she said.

He nodded but looked ready to pass out.

"Hold on," she said to him as she helped hoist him up so he could walk out of the elevator, through the lobby and out the front door.

The two blocks to their apartment felt like it took forever to walk. She let him lean on her as she shielded the blood from view. He left a few bright red dots on the sidewalk as they journeyed back.

Once inside, he slumped to the floor with his back against the door. Ree immediately jumped into action, texting Grappell to send a doctor and then searching for anything she could use to clean up Quint and stop the bleeding.

"Stay with me, Quint," she said, tapping his cheek as his head rolled from side to side. "You're going to be okay. Got it?"

He didn't respond and she hoped it was because he was conserving energy and not because he was losing consciousness. She couldn't take off his shirt fast enough. Her fingers fumbled with the buttons. Her hands trembled as adrenaline faded. The bandage below his ribs was soaked in blood. What had those animals done to him?

Her skin crawled at the memory of Vadik's hands on her. This was so much worse.

Yes, she was going to enjoy locking that jerk and his cohorts behind bars and throwing away the key. But Quint needed to live long enough to see it happen. Longer than that to be with her and figure out where this thing that kept growing between them would decide to take them.

Ree peeled the bandage off his left side. His hands came up to hers and his eyes blinked open as he winced. He curled forward.

"I'm sorry," Ree said quietly. "I don't mean to hurt you. I need to get something to stop the bleeding."

She hopped up to her feet and bolted into the bathroom. After retrieving a couple of clean hand towels, she hurried back to a slumped-over Quint. His skin had an ashen quality that sent her stress levels soaring.

"You're going to be fine," she said, mostly for her own benefit even though she hoped he could hear her.

His slight nod said he was hanging in there.

"A doctor is on the way," she reassured him. "I have to stop the bleeding, and this might hurt. Stay strong for me, okay?"

Without waiting for a response, she folded a hand towel and pressed it against his wound. Quint sat bolt upright. If he was feeling pain, he was still alive. She took it as a promising sign even though she hated hurting him.

A knock at the door came at the same time as a text. This must be the doctor. Thank heaven they were in a major city. She'd been on assignments in the country where there wasn't a doctor on standby.

A quick peek through the peephole confirmed her suspicions. She eased Quint away from the door and then opened it. Her cell started buzzing like crazy and she figured it was Grappell trying to get ahold of her to get a status update on Quint.

"Come on in, Doctor," she said, glancing at the name stitched above the pocket of his lab coat. Ramirez.

At this point, Quint was lying on his side, curled up. She could only imagine the beating he'd taken once he'd left the penthouse. At least the two of them hadn't been made. The case wasn't a total loss, even though she couldn't imagine going back there.

End of the line?

It might very well be for Quint. His injuries looked severe before the beating. Now? She couldn't imagine how the man could keep going. He'd barely made it this far and had lost a lot of blood. He'd barely made it to their apartment before sliding down the door and settling onto the floor.

Dr. Ramirez went right to work as Ree washed the blood off her hands and then checked her cell phone. The messages coming in weren't from Grappell at all. They were from Bjorn.

If she told their boss what was really happening with Quint, she would remove him from the case. Backing out now would do enormous damage after the progress they'd made. Being honest with their boss would erase all the hard work Quint had done up to this point.

If only there was a way to ask him what he wanted her to do about Bjorn. Talking to their boss without him felt like going behind his back. Doing so would damage the trust they'd built.

Should she risk everything between them personally and do it for the sake of the case?

Chapter Nineteen

For the next forty-eight hours, Quint was in and out of consciousness. Most of the time was a blur, except that he remembered being taken out of the apartment on a gurney and then returned in a wheelchair. Every time he opened his eyes, Ree was there, just as she was now as she sat staring out the window.

"I had a nightmare that I got in a fight," he said. His voice seemed to catch her off guard.

"Quint. You're awake," she said, immediately moving to his side. She perched on the bed and took his hand in hers.

"I'm still kicking." He made a move to sit up and concern wrinkled her forehead. She wore a weary expression, like someone who had been to hell and back from worry.

"Good. I happen to like you that way," she said with a forced smile. It didn't reach her eyes but he was grateful for the attempt. The news from the doctor must not have been great over the last few days.

"I was out for two days," he said, easing up to sitting.

"How do you know?" she asked.

"I counted the number of times the sun went down," he stated. He was surprisingly not thirsty but had a tacky taste in his mouth. Right. He hadn't brushed his teeth in all that time.

"Can I get you anything?" she asked. "The doctor had me order power bars in case you woke up hungry."

"One might be nice but I can't put anything in my mouth until I brush my teeth," he admitted. He made a move to get up and the room started spinning.

"You might want to slow down there, mister," she warned, her tone lighter now but still cautious.

"Where's the fun in that?" he quipped.

"At least your sense of humor is intact," she responded. "Hold on. I'll get a toothbrush."

Ree disappeared into the bathroom and then came back with supplies. "You get started brushing and I'll grab a bowl along with a cup of water."

"You might be an angel," he said.

"Hold on to that thought." She disappeared again, returning at the same time he started brushing. Her timing had always been spot-on. She set the bowl on his lap and held on to the water cup.

Brushing his teeth made him feel like he might have died and gone to heaven. It was always the little things he took for granted every day that seemed so huge when they were taken away. Once he'd thoroughly rinsed, he tugged Ree toward him.

"What?" The concern wrinkle came back.

"Okay if I kiss you?" he asked and his stomach tied

in knots, as if he was suddenly in high school asking out the prom queen.

"I'd like that a lot," she said, leaning into him until their lips gently touched. She pulled back quickly. "I don't want to hurt you."

"Thank you for taking care of me, Ree."

She smiled.

"Let me get something for you to eat," she said, brushing right past his thank-you.

"I mean it, Ree. You're an amazing person and partner. I hit the jackpot with you and I can't imagine doing this with anyone else," he said in all honesty.

A mix of emotions passed behind those emerald eyes.

"What is it?" he asked, picking up on something. She was hiding information. And it immediately dawned on him what it was. "Is Bjorn pulling you from the case?"

"Me?" she asked. "No."

Before he could ask another question, she held up a hand and hurried out of the room. By the time she returned ten minutes later, the smell of fresh-brewed coffee had him sitting all the way up.

Ree set two mugs on the nightstand and then produced a couple of power bars.

"They taste a little bit like mud, but a lot of protein is packed in there," she said, taking a seat and peeling open hers.

"Could be worse," he said, then locked gazes with her. "Tell me. How much worse is it for me?"

Ree issued a sharp sigh.

"Bjorn wants you off the case," she admitted.

"I should have seen that coming," he said. "How long do I have to convince her or is the paperwork already in process?"

"It was, but I managed to hold her at bay once you got a text that said you're needed for a job in two days," she said.

"And Bjorn went for it?" He had to admit that he was more than a little surprised.

"Not at first, but I convinced her that you'd made a lot of progress with Vadik in a short amount of time. Giselle said so, too. I used it to push an agenda that I knew you wanted. But that isn't to say I feel good about doing it, Quint."

A storm clouded those green eyes.

"If you could have seen what you looked like when I got you home..." She stopped speaking and just stared at the rim of the coffee cup she picked up. It wasn't like Ree to cry, but he suspected tears were the reason she tucked her chin to her chest and refused to look at him directly.

"I'm fine now," he said. "The food and caffeine will help."

"I just don't know if continuing on the case right now is the best idea," she said on a shrug.

"Thank you for not agreeing with Bjorn." If she had, he wouldn't be in this room right now. He'd be in the hospital, and then would eventually be released after a medical evaluation only to find himself sitting at a desk for another six months or longer. "You're right about the progress. We'd lose ground if we pulled out of the case now. Who knows when we'll get this close again?"

"Is it worth your life, though?"

There was a time not all that long ago when he would have answered a resounding yes. Quint had gone to sleep thinking about how much he'd let down Tessa and her baby, and woken up missing his best friend so badly he ached. Some people would have said the two of them should have gotten married. There were worse things in a marriage than to be best friends. He'd offered, half-jokingly, when she'd told him about the pregnancy. He'd almost convinced her that everyone would just believe the child was his, anyway, considering their closeness wasn't exactly a secret.

Tessa had touched his hand and told him that she could never allow him to settle for her when he would never love her. And then something in her eyes—something he'd chalked up to pregnancy hormones at the time—had made him believe she might have crossed an emotional line and fallen for him.

She'd whipped out all the lines, like he deserved better and that he would find someone he couldn't live without some day. He'd told her, honestly, that he didn't want to live without her.

They both knew they weren't talking about the same kind of love. He'd explained that he did love her and there was no one he'd rather spend a Sunday afternoon with watching a game or going for a hike. She'd smiled—and that smile still haunted him—and told him how much she appreciated his friendship.

Tessa knew that he would do anything for her and that kid, even if it meant living the rest of his life with someone he loved but wasn't *in love* with. Quint had reached a point in life where he didn't believe he was capable. He'd dated a whole lot of people without finding the magic Tessa seemed so certain was out there waiting for him. Half of him believed if he hadn't found it by now, he never would. So he'd made the marriage offer.

Now, looking at Ree, he realized what he'd been missing all these years. But he had a responsibility to Tessa and her baby that would eat him alive if he tried to walk away from this case.

"I have to see this thing through," he said to Ree. He could only hope she understood his reasoning.

"OKAY," REE SAID. This wasn't the time to try to unpack everything bottling up inside her when it came to Quint Casey and his need for revenge. "I'll let Bjorn know you're good to keeping working."

"She'll trust your opinion," Quint said, taking a bite of the power bar.

"I know." She had so many mixed feelings about making the recommendation for him to continue. The thing she kept coming back to was wondering what she would do if the shoe was on the other foot. What if Shane or Finn, or one of her other brothers, had been killed by one of these bastards?

Ree would go to the ends of the earth to lock up the person responsible. So she couldn't fault Quint, but it was hard to be in love with him. She picked up her mug and took a sip of coffee. With her free hand, she reached for his. He threaded their fingers together.

"Thank you for sticking with me on this case," he said quietly.

"I'm not going to lie and say it's easy by any stretch of the imagination," she responded honestly. "But I have two days to get you in good enough shape to pick up where we left off a couple of nights ago. And I plan to do everything in my power to ensure you can get the evidence we need for a bust."

An emotion flickered behind Quint's eyes that she couldn't immediately read. And then it dawned on her.

"You don't care about putting Vadik behind bars, do you?" she asked.

"Not if it would scare away Dumitru," he admitted after a long pause.

"Think about what you might be doing," she said to Quint.

"I've had nothing but time to think," he stated. "The low-level guys can go down. It happens a lot because they are on the front lines. If I take Vadik down before getting to Dumitru, he'll spook."

"We'll go after him, Quint. We'll lock him up and throw away the key," Ree said. "But we have to eliminate each level of threat."

"I don't agree on this one, Ree," he said and then abruptly changed the subject. "What do you know about the Acura guy?"

She stared at him for a long moment, not exactly

ready to move on but also realizing when a battle wasn't worth fighting.

After taking a deep breath, she started in. "I looked at the file. The name on his ID was Timothy Challan. He has ties to Christian Moffo, who has loose ties with Vadik."

Quint nodded.

"Do you know where the jeans I had on are?" he asked.

"As a matter of fact, I do." She set down her coffee mug and retrieved what he was actually looking for—the folded-up piece of paper he kept inside his pocket. She grabbed a pen before he asked, knowing full well he wanted to jot down the new name and link on the tree he'd created.

She handed over the paper and pen before reclaiming her seat. As expected, he made the note.

"How are you feeling?" she asked, really looking at him. His coloring was coming back and he had a whole lot more life in his expression than in the last forty-eight hours.

"I've been better," he quipped, leaning back against the headboard. He lifted his mug. "This is a huge help. Otherwise, I feel like I've been run over by a Mack truck."

"You kind of were," she said with a slow exhale.

"Chef," he said, drawing a few lines from Vadik's name. He wrote the names Keith and Samuel underneath Chef's.

"He must be fairly high up if he's calling the shots," she said.

"I'm guessing the other night was an initiation if they already reached out to give me work," he said.

"I figured," she admitted.

"What's your impression of Vadik?" he asked.

"Other than being a dirty criminal who also happens to be a chauvinist pig?" She arched an eyebrow. "There isn't much to like about him."

"He's slick," Quint said. "It'll be hard to get evidence against him because I doubt he gets his hands dirty at his level."

Ree nodded her agreement. "He has an entourage around him at all times from what I can tell. Giselle is afraid of him and also seems to have a healthy respect for him."

"What about her? Is she trustworthy?" he asked.

"She seems loyal to Axel, but who really knows," she said. "I would trust any one of these people about as much as I can throw them and she hasn't exactly stopped by to see if you are okay or check on me."

"Challan had duct tape and rope in the Acura," she said, circling back to their earlier conversation.

"Pretty much makes him guilty as sin," he stated.

"He wasn't able to get to Axel's family, but they were able to get him on attempted murder charges with your statement," she said.

Quint nodded.

At full strength, she had no doubt he could take on any one of these jerks. Injured? She worried.

"What do you think about the two of us taking off for a few days? Maybe a week?" she asked. "We could always say I had to go back to Seattle to see my sister."

He shook his head. She figured he wouldn't agree but it had been worth a shot.

"Is he out?" he asked. "Challan?"

"We lucked out because he was out on parole, so he'll be locked up for a long time," she said. "He's out of the picture for a while."

"Good. I don't need to run in to him again or have him on the outside looking for me," he stated. "In fact, now that I'm thinking about it, Chef mentioned something about me being in jail while Keith and Samuel took a baseball bat to me."

Now it was Ree's turn to wince.

"It only felt like one," he said with a smirk. "I'm pretty sure they only kicked and punched me."

"You couldn't fight back," she said. "It wasn't fair."

"Initiations never are," he stated. "At first, I was afraid they'd made me. But then I realized I had to strap on for the ride. If I'd fought back, they probably would have killed me and then dropped me in the Trinity River."

"In your condition, you wouldn't have been able to do much damage to them, anyway," she said on a sigh.

"We got through it." He threaded their fingers again. Then he brought the back of her hand up to his lips and pressed a tender kiss there.

Her stomach dropped and her chest squeezed. It would be so easy to go down that road again with Quint. The same question haunted her: where would it lead?

Chapter Twenty

Two days of nothing but food, rest and the gym had Quint raring to go. The assignment came down from Chef and meant he'd be working side by side with Keith and Samuel. Not exactly a warm and fuzzy thought after the beating in the alley, but he'd take the progress toward Vadik and, ultimately, Dumitru.

"I wish I could be there," Ree said as Quint shrugged into a black T-shirt. His all-dark outfit would fade into the background.

"Believe me, I'd like it if you had my back rather than Keith or Samuel, but that's not an option here," he stated.

"On some level, I do know that," she replied. "You'll be wearing a wire and I'll be around as soon as I can get away from the party."

Vadik was stuck in the Dark Ages when it came to how to treat the opposite sex. He seemed to believe women were nothing more than arm candy meant to give him something pretty to look at.

"Shame you can't fake a headache," he said, attaching the safety pin that was actually a listening device to the inside of his shirt.

"I noticed Security at the penthouse door barely patted Giselle down the first time I was there," Ree stated. "Once you're in, they probably get more lax."

"Still, be careful," he said. "If they see the earpiece disguised as an earring—"

"That's not going in until I'm out of there," she said, putting her hands up in the surrender position. "Did Chef give you any idea of where you might be headed?"

"No." Quint shook his head. "All I know is that we'll be responsible for 'product' that will be brought to an empty warehouse in the warehouse district until it's loaded and onto its next destination. That's pretty much all I'm being told right now."

"A babysitting job," she said.

"I imagine we'll be helping unload and then load. They must change vehicles while in transit," he continued.

"Makes sense. Moving the product to a different vehicle every so often would lessen the chances of getting caught," she said. "The trucks only have to weigh in at certain intervals. What happens in between is impossible to track."

"Exactly right. We've seen it before. It's slow and methodical," he stated.

"Which also makes me believe it's a large load," she said.

"I can't help but wonder if some of it isn't going to be offloaded here in the Dallas area," he added.

"This is a big market for weapons," she said. "Despite being able to buy a gun easily in the state."

"We all know they want to get around a paper trail," he said with another nod.

"That's just what this city needs. More weapons that can't be traced back to an individual," she said on a sigh.

Quint finished buttoning the last button of his shirt and then locked gazes with Ree, who was sitting on the bathroom counter, facing him.

"This is as good as it gets," he said, motioning toward his reflection in the mirror.

"Looks pretty great from where I sit," she quipped, and her cheeks turned a few shades of red. "The shirt. It's nice. That's what I mean."

Quint leaned a little closer until his lips pressed against hers. For the last two days, neither one of them brought up their relationship status, or where they thought it was going. They were important questions and they deserved answers. For now, it was nice just to spend time together. He'd missed holding her at night and waking up with her hair spilled out across the pillow. He'd missed her warm body tangled with his. And he'd missed the easy way they had with each other. Neither had to work for conversation. In fact, Quint had never considered himself the chatty type until Ree. Color him shocked that he had a hard time sleeping at night because he wanted to hear more about her childhood. Growing up with four brothers, she had stories. No matter how much she tried to convince him otherwise, it was easy to see how much she loved every single one of them.

"I could stay here all night," he said, his lips moving against hers.

"We've covered that ground, mister. Back to work," she teased, leaning back until she rested against the mirror.

"In case I didn't tell you earlier, you're beautiful," he said.

The blush came back.

"I'm pretty sure you already said that half a dozen times tonight," she said with a smile that threatened to break down all of his defenses. "And yet it never gets old."

"Good. Because I plan to say it a whole lot more," he said as his phone buzzed in the next room. "We should probably head out."

She nodded.

"I see how these top criminals live and, sometimes—no, all the time—think the good guys should definitely get paid more than we do," Ree said, pushing off the counter. The sleek black silk bodysuit hugged her curves and showed off long legs. She had on a jade necklace that brought out the green in her eyes and caused his heart to detonate. "For instance, take Vadik living in the penthouse. That has to cost a pretty penny."

"I'm sure it does." Quint flicked off the bathroom light as they exited and moved toward the living room/kitchen area.

"Funny thing is, you couldn't pay me to live in a

penthouse downtown no matter how great Dallas might be for some," she said. "I couldn't be happier than when I'm home, sitting outside with a cup of coffee in the morning as the sun's coming up. There's no better view than watching the sun rise above the trees to the east on my property."

"You have a beautiful home, Ree. You found a piece of paradise here on earth and bought it with your own money," he said. "You should be very proud of what you've accomplished."

She stopped and planted a kiss on his lips at the door.

"Thank you, Quint," she said. "You're the first person to say those words to me."

"I'm sure your family means them, too," he said. "It's easy to see how much they love you."

"My brothers and grandfather? Yes. My mother—"

"Just doesn't know how to show it," he interrupted. "She leads with her worry when she should tell you what an amazing woman you are." She needed to know the truth. He'd seen a whole lot of love in the form of concern from her mother. Was she going about their relationship the wrong way? Absolutely. He wouldn't defend her there. And yet it was easy to see just how tight the family was. And her mother wouldn't worry at all if she didn't come from a place of caring.

Ree caught his gaze. "My brother Shane has been telling me the same thing for years. Why is it so hard to believe?"

"I think you have to look inside yourself for the answer to that question," he said to her.

"She has been so critical of me," she stated.

"There's no excuse for it," he agreed. "It undermines all the love she has for you."

Ree concurred, then pressed a tender kiss to his lips. "Thank you for not defending her or hating her. Most seem to fall into one camp or the other," she said. "There hasn't been a whole lot of middle ground when it comes to mine and my mother's relationship."

"Family is complicated," he said with a shrug. "I'm the last one to known how to handle them."

"They can be a handful but I wouldn't trade any one of them for the world," she said with a smile that cracked more of his defenses.

"They're lucky to have you," he said, then whispered, "And so am I."

She must not have heard him because she pulled back and said, "It's party time."

THE WALK TO the penthouse was short and quiet. Ree knew she would be hooked into Quint the entire time with the earring and yet being physically away from each other was going to be hard. What if he needed backup? It was just the two of them on this fact-finding mission.

The last place she wanted to be was at the penthouse with Vadik when the real work was being done in the field by Quint. It gave her a new appreciation for what Quint must have been feeling on their last two cases, when she had to work as first a waitress in a restaurant/bar and then at a popular Houston nightspot for the well-off. Those undercover assignments had led them to this point.

Ree was uncomfortable walking around in these heels, and she was grumpy. At least she would be able to listen to Quint the entire time he was gone.

Giselle met them both at the front door of Vadik's building. She gave each a quick hug, then said, "Chef is expecting you around back. He said you'd know where to meet him."

Quint nodded before giving Ree a kiss that threatened to melt all her defenses. She was having a difficult enough time thinking about when this case would end and she would go back to her normal life.

A thought struck her, out of the blue. She was done with undercover work. Ree set it aside. She'd been contemplating whether or not she wanted to stay on the job recently. What surprised her was the finality of it. A decision had been made and now it was just about working out the details, the timing, and what she planned to do next.

This career path had played out for her and it was time to make some hard decisions. She had some money saved. Could she take time off to figure out her next move?

Ree shelved the thought and grabbed Giselle's arm.

"We should probably get upstairs," she said, shaking off a foreboding feeling that suddenly came over her. It was a heavy gray cloud that showed up on a perfect day, hovering over her and thickening the air around her, making it hard to breathe.

"How is he really feeling?" Giselle asked.

"It wouldn't matter," she responded. "He needs the work so he was going to be here no matter what."

Ree held on to Giselle for the elevator ride to the penthouse, keeping her eyes squeezed shut for most of it. Being in the city reminded her how deeply she wished she was home instead. A few deep breaths later and the elevator dinged. Thankfully.

She opened her eyes and practically jumped out. From the corner of her eye, she caught Giselle smiling.

"I'll never get used to heights," Ree admitted.

"We all have something to get over, right?" Giselle said. She squeezed Ree's hand. "You did great."

After walking inside and being patted down, Ree was escorted to the balcony. *Great.* She did realize being near Vadik would make it easier to figure out how to get to Dumitru. The faster she could hand over the information to Quint, the quicker this whole nightmare would end.

Vadik nodded to her escort. Giselle walked Ree over to him.

"Thank you, Gigi," he said and Giselle seemed to take the hint she was supposed to exit the area.

She retreated with a quick glance at Ree.

There were two men standing with Vadik and three others leaning on the wall or sitting on a chair. Twice as many women milled around, looking like accessories.

"Come closer," Vadik said to Ree.

She did.

"I owe you an apology," he began, surprising her with the line of thought.

"Why is that?" she asked, cocking an eyebrow.

"My associates became a little too enthusiastic the other night," he said. She glanced down at his fingers, which were braided in front of him, and imagined all the blood on those hands.

Through her earpiece, she heard the low hum of a vehicle's engine on what sounded like a highway. There was music playing in the background, too, some kind of rap.

"He was pretty banged-up," she agreed. "Said he tripped on the way downstairs."

Vadik's eyes widened and he clamped his mouth shut. He must not have been expecting a response like that one. "I'm afraid my guys might have helped him along when they should have stopped him from hitting the ground."

"He's feeling better now," she said nonchalantly, throwing in a shrug for effect. He seemed to be buying her routine. Violence was part of the deal in a life of crime. Initiations could be brutal and sometimes led to death. As far as she was concerned, Quint had made it out alive and therefore was successful. The fact that she'd had to wear ridiculously tight and form-fitting clothing on their last two assignments paled in comparison to what he'd been through two days ago. The other problem was that he was now in a weakened state. Fighting back would be that much more difficult.

That she hadn't heard him speak after the initial

greeting with Keith and Samuel didn't help. At least he had his phone with him. On it was an encrypted tracking app that no one would be able to detect. Once Quint got home, they could pull it up and retrace the trail. It would make it easier for Quint so he could focus on what was happening with Keith and Samuel rather than worry about memorizing landmarks. Although, knowing Quint, he was doing that, too.

"That's good to hear," Vadik said. She could tell he was feeling her out. There was no way to tell if she'd truly passed or not. If she made a mistake on her end, it could cost Quint's life. Being on this side of the equation and out of the direct action was even more stressful than she realized.

Giselle reappeared. Vadik nodded.

Ree could only hope it meant she'd done okay.

Chapter Twenty-One

The vehicle stopped in front of a warehouse on the outskirts of Dallas. Quint had only been in the SUV for twenty-three minutes, according to his cell phone, from the time they left downtown Dallas to reaching their destination to the north. Much to his surprise, they'd pulled into the back of a jewelry import shop on Harry Hines Boulevard.

"We have a shipment coming in and we have to sit on it for a while," Keith said.

Quint involuntarily fisted his hands, wishing he could throw a few punches to get Keith and Samuel back for the other night. Forcing his fingers to open again, he tucked his cell inside his pocket and exited the white Suburban. It was already dark outside. The sun had just descended. And yet, it was still hot enough to make him sweat through his button-down.

"We'll just throw the assets in the back here, like usual." Samuel unlocked the back door of the warehouse-style building.

He flipped on a light and the three of them filed in.

This looked like a regular office area. A wall of shelves caught Quint's eye. This area should be larger. He took note and followed Keith and Samuel.

"This door here leads to the showroom," Keith said. He tried the handle and opened it a crack. "We keep it closed while we're working back here so no one can see us from the front window."

"Got it," Quint stated.

"Bathroom is over here." Keith pointed to another closed door. "And this is where we keep the assets." He walked over to the shelves and moved a stack of books. He punched in a code and the shelves came toward him.

Quint stood at the mouth of the room. There were three mattresses scattered on the floor. A commode and sink gave the place a prison feel. It hit him immediately there was a whole lot more than gunrunning going on in there. Could be fugitives. Hiding them with guns could keep them underground for long periods.

But his mind snapped to a different place when he saw a box of toys in the corner. Human trafficking. These were the most difficult cases. He didn't need to have children of his own to feel sick at the thought of young girls being sold into the sex trade. It was almost incomprehensible to him that crimes like that occurred in the twentieth-first century, except experience had taught him the trade was alive, well and prospering.

Still made him want to vomit.

"Make yourself at home," Keith said. "We might be here a while."

"Is this driver good?" Quint asked.

"We don't get into that side of the business," Keith said, exchanging a look with Samuel.

"Hey, I just got out. I need to make sure I'm not working with amateur hour here," Quint protested. "I go back in and I'm not seeing my wife in a very long time."

"Don't worry about her," Keith said with a whistle. "I'll keep her warm until you get out."

"I hate to break the news to you but if I go down, there's a real good chance the three of us go down together," Quint said, acting nonplussed even though he really wanted to put his fist through Keith's crooked teeth.

"The driver better check out," Keith said. "But I don't have any control over that side of the business."

The idea of going to jail didn't seem to sit well with Keith. Good. Because the bastard was going down if Quint had anything to say about it. And he did. There was circumstantial evidence here. Not enough to put Keith away.

The sound of a truck pulling up to the back got Keith off the internet, where he'd been going back and forth between watching preseason football and finding a new place to live. Apparently, he was in the market for a two-bedroom apartment somewhere downtown that was close to Vadik but not in the same building. For one, he said he couldn't afford it. The other reason was that he didn't want to run in to Vadik downstairs at the gym. Work was one thing, Keith had explained. He liked to keep his personal life separate.

Quint couldn't wait to find out exactly what kind

of shipment they were receiving. Until a frightened-looking young girl was hustled into the room. She couldn't have been more than eleven or twelve years old. She was followed by another kid close to her age. Then another. The small room filled with half a dozen girls in a matter of minutes.

Next came the weapons. There were five four-by-eight-foot crates. All locked. All set inside the room with the girls, giving them even less room. The first girl had the biggest pair of round, scared eyes—eyes that looked like they were ready to pop out of her head. She was in so much shock that she didn't speak, most likely couldn't if she'd tried. Everything seemed to be happening around her instead of to her. She'd checked out mentally and emotionally in a big way.

Quint knew right then, without a doubt, he couldn't let this girl be sold into a system that caused his stomach to churn just thinking about it. Even if it meant losing the trail to Dumitru. Tessa would not want Quint to allow these children to be treated and sold like pieces of furniture, as if their lives had no value. She would be disappointed in him if he didn't do everything he could to put a stop to this transaction.

Which meant pulling a bust way before he'd intended. Quint cursed underneath his breath. The kid with the bug eyes and stringy blond hair would haunt him. He'd planned on holding off on initiating a bust so he could use Vadik to get closer to Dumitru. A bust this soon would ruin his chances. And yet, it couldn't be helped. He would schedule a raid. It was the only choice.

"Get food and feed the assets," Keith said.

It took everything inside Quint not to correct Keith by saying, *do you mean the little girls?* Rage boiled inside his veins that someone could be so callous when talking about children.

There were five girls with varying shades of dark hair, and the blonde. For some reason, she hit him the hardest. Was it because she looked like a miniature version of Tessa? Or did he imagine Tessa's baby might look like the kid?

More of that rage filled him and it took all his willpower to calm down before he was noticed. He helped carry in the last crate as Samuel sat on the desk chair, spinning around like an eight-year-old, eating an apple. The fruit was probably meant for the kids.

Keith checked his cell phone. He cursed as he closed and locked the back door.

"What's wrong? Is the next truck going to be late with pickup?" Samuel asked.

Quint knew better than to say a word. First of all, his anger was bubbling dangerously close to the surface. He couldn't allow it to spill over, and there was only so much he could take. This seemed like a good time to remind himself of the jail time coming for these guys, and that he and Ree would save these kids so they could be reunited with their families.

The blond girl had dirt on her face and a tattered bow in her hair. It was an image he wouldn't soon forget.

Quint knew full well the trail to Dumitru might stop right here, so he looked at the young girl one more time.

She drew back under his scrutiny. He wanted to offer some reassurance to her and the others. He wanted to let them know he wasn't there to hurt them. That he was the good guy. And he wanted to tell them he would find their families if it was the last thing he ever did. But they were in shock. A couple of them had huddled together, clinging to each other as if their lives depended on it. Trauma could do that to someone. His heart went out to these kiddos. They'd clearly been through more than any kid this age should have to go through.

Keith stared at his phone.

"One of the clients is trying to back out of the sale," Keith said. "We need to pay him a visit."

"I'll grab the tire iron." Samuel rubbed his hands together.

Quint tensed before forcing himself to breathe. He relaxed his shoulders.

"You wait here with the merch," Keith said to him. "We'll handle this."

"Who is it this time?" Samuel asked.

"A judge in Plano," Keith stated. "Chef is sending the address."

So far, Quint could link human and weapons trafficking to Vadik's business. But any lawyer worth his salt would be able to get Vadik off the hook by saying he wasn't aware of what was happening with his business.

"Stick around and make sure these are ready to go," Keith said, motioning toward the kids.

"Will do, chief," Quint said. He managed to get out the words without gritting his teeth.

Despite knowing he would get these kids to safety, he couldn't say a word to any of them. Not yet. Not after the ordeal they'd been through. They might not believe him, anyway. Who knew what had been promised to them, or the manner in which they'd been separated from their families?

The minute Keith and Samuel were out of the building, he moved to the fridge. There were stacks of Lunchables inside, along with juice boxes. He started passing them out as the kids huddled together on one of the mattresses.

One thing was certain—Vadik was pure evil. The jewelry import shop made for an easy way to launder money. The North Dallas location made for an easy hub to move product throughout the country. Merchandise could split three ways from here.

After handing out food, he gave them drinks. There were water bottles in the fridge as well, so he passed those out.

"If anyone needs to use the restroom, there's a better one out here," he said, wishing he could call Ree. If his mouth moved while talking toward the wire and he wasn't in conversation with anyone, suspicion could be raised. There could be a camera hidden somewhere in the place. He had to play it cool. Being obvious about looking for it would only tip off Vadik's guys. Chef could be watching. He seemed to be in charge.

Quint coughed into his elbow, covering his mouth. In the few seconds it happened, he said, "Send the troops. Watch for Keith and Samuel. Nail all those bastards."

He could only hope she'd heard him. And now, all he could do was wait for Keith and Samuel to return.

REE HAD LOST contact with Quint. Fear gripped her that Keith and Samuel might have taken him somewhere to kill him this time. Vadik didn't give her the impression he was any the wiser about their undercover status. But he was slick.

Since she'd heard background noise earlier, she assumed the electronic devices had been working. It was possible Quint was in an area that cut off reception. They were using cell towers, just like with a phone.

"How long have you been together?" Giselle asked Ree as they munched on snacks at the granite island.

"Eight years," Ree said, figuring they'd be busted if someone was on the other side asking Quint the same questions. "How about you and Axel?"

"Almost five years," she said.

Ree wondered if half the reason Axel cheated on his wife was to get a boy. Some guys were in to that macho stuff and this crowd seemed ripe for that particular brand of old-fashioned thinking.

Where was Quint?

She wanted to check her phone to see if location was a problem, but couldn't with Chef in this room. While Quint was healing, he'd told her every detail about the incident from a few nights ago. He probably wasn't strong enough to be out there doing whatever it was they had him doing.

Ree was seriously whipping herself into a frenzy.

"Relax," Giselle said quietly. "He'll be back." With her back to Chef, she made eyes at Ree.

This probably wasn't the time to point out the fact Giselle couldn't possibly know if that was true. Being nervous wasn't going to help.

"You're right," Ree said. "It's just he spent two days in bed after the last time he left with those two. And he was back before now."

"Initiations are hard. A whole lot don't come back to the penthouse after the first night," Giselle explained. "But your guy did. And now he'll be part of the crew. It might take time but he can work his way up. There's a real career here."

Ree smiled and nodded. Giselle seemed to have bought in to the whole nine yards. She'd gone in hook, line and sinker. Now, Ree questioned whether or not Giselle would leave once her part was done and WITSEC showed. She seemed married to this life. The best hope to go along with Axel's wishes was the possibility of getting her son back. It had been clear she loved him and didn't want him to stay at her sister's. But then, she'd also gotten used to the freedom that came with not having him around.

As much as Ree didn't want to admit it, not everyone could be saved. A person had to want it and Giselle looked mighty comfortable here at the penthouse. "Do you come here every night?"

"Mostly." Giselle lifted a shoulder like she was more than a little put off by the question.

"Just wondering what my life might have just

changed to," Ree said. She walked over to Giselle and took her arm. "It's amazing here."

"I know. Right?" Giselle's enthusiasm was back.

"What should we do next?" Ree asked, hoping there was something going on to kill the time until Quint returned or enough time had passed for her to go home. She had no idea what the courtesy wait limit was or if Quint would be coming back tonight at all.

"We could get a room," Giselle said and gave a look that Ree recognized as being hit on.

She immediately withdrew her hand from Giselle's. The act of touching clearly didn't mean the same thing to Giselle that it did to Ree. On Ree's side, it was innocent contact. Maybe to Giselle, being with a woman didn't feel like cheating.

"Or we could grab a glass of wine and eat a little more," Ree offered.

Giselle gave a nod of disappointment. She looked defeated.

"I'm sorry if I gave you the wrong impression," Ree said. "Quint and me have barely been back together after not seeing each other in a few years. It wouldn't seem right for me to be with you while he's out there trying to rebuild our life."

Ree hoped the explanation would float because she'd come up with it on the fly.

"Right. Makes sense," Giselle said, sounding a little less hurt by the rejection.

When did dating and being in relationships get so complicated? All Ree wanted at this point was someone to come home to every night. Someone like Quint, whom she couldn't wait to see so she could share all the good news. And someone who had broad enough shoulders to lean on when times got tough. She fully expected the support to be a two-way street, too.

Quint's voice came through. Ree toyed with the strap of her purse as she listened. Was he asking for help?

Chapter Twenty-Two

An hour passed. Then another. Finally, a vehicle pulled in the back. Quint hoped it was Keith and Samuel, but he prepared himself to see pretty much anything walk through the door. The voices on the other side belonged to them, and he breathed a sigh of relief.

Again, he coughed so he could send the signal for help.

The kids had settled down, clinging to each other as sleep eventually tugged them under. The little blonde sat in front of the pack, legs and arms folded, with her shoulders hunched forward as she played with the seam of a well-used blanket.

Quint's heart squeezed at the fact this little girl who should be out playing kickball, or with her Barbie dolls, was in a defensive position, ready to fight. Her arms were spindly, so she wouldn't be able to do much. But her small size didn't seem to matter to her. She sat there as though on point.

Keith came inside first, followed by Samuel.

"Did you get it taken care of?" Quint asked them.

Keith nodded. When Quint looked down at Samuel's right fist, he saw blood. The first thing Samuel did was walk to the bathroom. The sink turned on next. Quint cursed at the fact that evidence was being washed down the drain.

It was okay, he reminded himself. A good forensic tech would be able to corroborate Quint's story. There would be blood in the Suburban, enough DNA to retrace the steps and confirm what had happened. A judge in Plano had been beaten up. He would either call in sick tomorrow or show up battered and bruised.

Samuel was relentless once he locked on. The guy seemed to derive a sick pleasure from beating someone to a pulp. If Chef hadn't been there to intervene, Quint had no idea how far the man would have gone with him the other night. Too far?

The next thing Quint knew, the back door opened and something was tossed inside. Smoke started filling the room. Samuel cursed.

"It's a raid," he shouted and then started coughing.

"What do we do with the merch?" Quint said to Samuel.

"Do whatever the hell you want. It's every man for himself right now," Samuel said before climbing onto the desk. He pushed open one of the squares in the ceiling as Quint heard the littles in the next room start to cough.

"Vadik won't appreciate losing his merchandise," Quint said, knowing full well the team would have thrown a listening device inside along with the smoke bomb.

He pulled his shirt up over his nose and mouth to breathe as Keith joined Samuel on the desk. The guy hoisted himself up and into the opening in the ceiling. Keith quickly followed. Then, Samuel's head popped through the opening.

"Are you coming, man?" he asked.

"I'll find another way out," he said. "Go on."

There was no way he was leaving the kids inside alone. Plus, he needed to break away from Keith and Samuel if he was going to have a chance to get away.

"Keys," he said to Samuel. A set came flying through the opening.

"Good luck, man," Samuel said, seeming to have a new respect for Quint.

"You, too." It literally hurt Quint to say that. The last thing he wanted was for Samuel or Keith to get away. Law enforcement should be waiting outside at all possible exits. But even if they escaped, their DNA was all over the place.

The next thing he knew, something was being poured out of the opening. And then he heard the strike of a match. A second later, he saw the flames.

Quint cursed as he realized Keith and Samuel were torching the place.

Now, he really had to get the kids out. He bolted across the room, using the cloth of his shirt to cover his mouth and nose as best he could. He kicked the can toward the front of the room, in the opposite direction of the door he intended to walk through.

"Come on," he said, rounding up the half-dozen kids. "We have to get out of here."

Bug Eyes stared at him in disbelief but she did exactly as he said, gathering up the others to make sure they followed directions.

"Let's go," he urged, realizing the place could really go up at any second.

Through flames, he led the kids to the back door.

"You guys go out first, okay?" he urged.

They formed a semicircle around him. There were agents waiting at the other side of the back door, as expected. Quint put his hands in the air and squatted down so he would be at eye level with the kids if they were facing him.

They fanned out and the little girl stepped forward as though speaking for all of them. When Quint saw his chance, he bolted to the left. The alley in general was dark. He was fit and a fast runner. Granted, he was in a weakened state. These agents didn't know him from Adam, and would arrest him if he was caught because they either weren't aware of his undercover status or wouldn't blow his cover. Either way, he had to make a move now or risk exposure.

The problem with arrest was that he would go to jail alongside Samuel and Keith. Quint would come out and have to disappear. He'd have to hide his face for years because he would be viewed as rolling over in jail. No one would be released with evidence this strong against him.

Quint's lungs burned and his ribs hurt but he pumped

his arms and legs as fast as they would go. An agent had broken off from the group at the door and given chase, as expected.

The kids had acted as human shields, allowing for Quint's exit. At least the kids were in safe hands now.

Quint tripped and nearly did a face-plant. He scrambled up onto all fours and then to his feet. Adrenaline was the only reason he was still moving at this point. The pain would set in later. At least the kids were going home.

He dipped right and then left, pushing his way into a bar and a throng of people. Quint took an accidental elbow to the ribs as he weaved in and out of people around the bar. Thump. Thump. Thump. The bass vibrated through him as he crossed the small but packed dance floor.

Since running through the back and out the door would be expected, he made a circle and then exited out the front. His plan worked and he was free from the agent who'd been chasing him. He immediately unbuttoned his shirt, took it off and threw it inside a nearby dumpster. The agent believed he was chasing a guy in a black button-down. The initial visual was a strong one. Immediately changing his look would buy him time.

Music thumped from the row of dive bars on Harry Hines. A guy was dressed in black leather. Quint walked up to the tall shirtless, suspender-wearing blond guy.

"Any chance you'd be willing to sell your hat?" Quint asked, pulling out his wallet. "I have two hundred dollars."

"Sold," the blond said. He took off the black faux leather captain's hat and handed it over with an ear-to-ear grin.

"Thank you." Quint handed over the money.

"I feel like I should be thanking you," the guy quipped, waving the two Benjamins in the air. "You know I bought that for twelve ninety-nine. Right?"

"I'd be happy to take some of my money back," Quint stated after putting on the hat. He stepped a little closer to the group as a squad car rolled past. The cops were no doubt looking for him.

"Not tonight," the man stated. "But if you come inside with us, the first round is on me."

The cop car kept going, shining a light in between buildings.

"I'm good," Quint stated, cutting through the group and walking in the opposite direction of the squad car.

REE STOOD AT the island, nibbling on fruit, cheese and crackers while praying for word from Quint. She started picking up occasional street noises in her earpiece and then could have sworn she'd heard clubbing music.

Ever since the rejection, Giselle had kept her distance. Ree had lost track of the woman and figured she might have found someone to go into "a room" with after hitting up Ree.

Chef had been in the kitchen most of the evening as well. Was that how he'd earned his nickname? And then cell phones started going off. A buzz of activity began, causing panic to well up inside her.

The next thing she knew, Chef was being summoned out on the balcony. Giselle appeared. Her lipstick was a little bit smeared and her hair a bit messy. From all appearances, she'd gone into a room with someone.

"What's going on?" Ree asked in a whisper.

"From the looks of it, there's been a raid," Giselle informed her. She made eyes at Ree, who took in a deep breath.

"I don't want to lose him again. He just got out," she said, using her cover to explain why tears sprang to her eyes. "They'll throw away the key this time."

"It'll be okay," Giselle stated. "We don't know what happened yet. There's no reason to panic. Stay calm."

It sounded like Giselle was trying to convince herself.

"If he got away, he won't come here. There's no way he would draw attention to Vadik," Ree said. "He would, however, go home. I need to go."

"Not right now, you don't," Giselle warned. There was something in her voice that rooted Ree to her spot. A threat?

"You're right. It would look bad if I got caught leaving the building. I'm sure the feds are watching," she said. "Seeing if anyone panics."

"They're always around somewhere, lurking," Giselle stated and a whole different side to her started shining through. This evening had been filled with surprises, twists and turns. Ree couldn't wait to get the hell away from this penthouse.

Right now, all she could think of was Quint's safety.

If he got arrested, there'd be no explaining why he was released. Neither of them would be able to show their faces around this crowd again. For Ree, the idea was appealing. She'd made a decision to wrap up her undercover career in favor of sleeping in her own bed seven nights a week. Zoey and the puppy had tugged at a heartstring Ree didn't realize was there. Change was good. Right? She was pushing forty years old. A number that caused plenty of people to rethink their strategy in life. Two of her older brothers had already hit the number, gotten married and started families. Finn, the youngest and closest in age to Ree, was in a long-term relationship. His fortieth was around the corner.

What was it about birthdays that ended with zeroes that had people feeling like they should be at a certain point in life?

"Jail would be the end of us," Ree continued, picking up the earlier thread. "I wouldn't make it through another stint and he'd be going away for much longer this time."

"You might surprise yourself. It's crazy what you'll do for love," Giselle said, pouring herself a fresh glass of wine. "Want one?"

"Why not," Ree stated. She'd been nursing the same drink all evening without taking more than two sips. She'd set it down somewhere and one of the arm-candy ladies had gone behind her and cleaned it up. Besides, she needed to look like she fit in and Giselle was drinking. Plus, it would give her something to do with her hands.

Giselle poured another glass and handed it over. Ree took a long pull before setting the glass on the granite.

Chef appeared in the doorway. His gaze was locked on to Ree and his expression told her bad news was coming.

Chapter Twenty-Three

"There have been two arrests," Chef stated. "And Vadik's workplace went up in flames."

"Do we have names?" Ree immediately asked.

Chef shook his head.

And then it dawned on her someone might have perished in the fire. "Did everyone get out of the building?"

"It seems so, but we can't be certain yet," Chef stated.

Ree picked up her wineglass and took another long pull. More than anything else, she wanted to go home. Leave here and she might seem too eager. Plus, she could miss out on information. But every fiber of her being wanted her to walk out that door and either head home or go for a drive to check the area. Quint could be lying in a ditch somewhere for all she knew.

Returning the glass to its spot, she wrung her hands together.

"Have you heard from your man?" Chef asked. At least, the recent turn of events gave her a reason to check her cell phone.

She pulled her phone from her purse and checked the

screen. Her heart gave an audible thud when there was nothing from Quint. She shook her head.

"You'll let us know if anything changes," he said, but it was more statement than question.

"I will," she said to Chef as Giselle moved beside Ree and then linked their arms. Ree must have shot a warning look because Giselle shrugged and made eyes that said she wasn't trying to hit on Ree.

Good. Because dating sure had become confusing. Ree took this as another sign she'd been out of the swing of things far too long. The thought of turning forty alone was enough to make her realize change was needed.

Right now, all she wanted to focus on was getting Quint home safely. The thought of leaving her job and finding a new career was gaining momentum, sounding better and better every time she thought about it.

And the first person she wanted to bounce the idea off of was Quint. The thought of never seeing him again threatened to pull her under and toss her around at the bottom of the ocean. Waiting was hard. Not knowing was hard. Being without Quint was hard.

A half hour passed with her standing at the island. The men inside hovered around Vadik. Ree knew an agent would be here at some point. After all, the jewelry import store that had been set on fire belonged to Vadik.

"I should probably head home," Ree finally said to Giselle when another fifteen minutes passed.

"It's probably good that we haven't heard anything yet," Giselle said with a smile that didn't reach her eyes. Did this bring back memories of when Axel was busted?

Speaking of which, Giselle would be going into witness protection soon with her son. It was odd knowing someone's life was about to change forever when they were oblivious. After the invitation to grab a room plus seeing how much Giselle seemed to fit right in here at the penthouse, Ree again questioned whether or not the woman would accept the offer.

"I guess," Ree finally answered. "I want to go just in case he shows up there. There's no telling what shape he'll be in and he must have lost his cell phone or I would have heard from him by now."

Giselle nodded as panic mounted inside Ree. For once, she didn't have to hide it and it felt good to be her authentic self for a change.

"Will you tell Chef that I left and that I'll let you know if I hear from him?" Ree asked, figuring she could sneak out by using the service elevator. She didn't want to think about what had happened the last time Quint had exited in the same manner. At least she would be alone.

"Sure," Giselle said with a look of sympathy. She, of all people, could relate to her boyfriend ending up in jail, or worse. Looking closer, Giselle's eyes had a dullness to them that said she'd been in this position before and realized she wouldn't always walk away from it.

"Stop over at the apartment when you think it's safe. Okay?" Ree asked. She needed to check in with Grappell before she told Giselle the real reason Axel had her bring Ree and Quint into the fold. There was something small and lost about the young woman now. Ree had a real weakness for those who had no one to look out for them in life.

"I promise to," Giselle stated with a forced-looking smile.

Ree could practically see the wheels turning in Giselle's mind. Was she concerned about being locked up, away from her son? Did this scenario remind her of the time Axel was busted? Ree had no idea what the young woman was thinking. All she knew for certain was that she needed to get home and check in with Grappell. Sticking around here was getting her nowhere. At the apartment, she could find out what the agents knew.

"Thanks," Ree said to Giselle before slipping out the back. She tapped her toe on the tile flooring, waiting for the elevator. It took its sweet time but finally made it. The trip down was quick. She exited into the alleyway where Quint had taken a beating a couple of nights ago. A cold chill raced down her back at the thought of what had happened as she made her way out of the alley and onto the street.

Ree barely made it to the opposite sidewalk as three vehicles she recognized as belonging to federal agents came roaring up. There were two SUVs and a white minivan. Three teams flooded the sidewalk, and all members wore navy blue windbreakers with their alphabet letters running across the back and another set on the sleeve.

Ree discreetly slipped her cell out of her purse as she made a beeline toward her apartment, keeping her head down the whole time. Being recognized by one of the agents wouldn't be ideal. Plus, the timing of her exit would cast her under suspicion with Vadik, and possibly get Quint killed. She managed to fire off a warning text about the bust to Giselle without drawing attention to herself by the agents.

A team entered the building as one positioned themselves in front. A third headed toward the alley. There must be solid evidence against Vadik. A link to the building wouldn't be enough to bring out this many teams unless Grappell had been able to arrange a warrant.

The buzz of her cell sent her heart rate soaring. She checked the screen and saw a response from Giselle. They must have crossed paths with their communication. Ree read the message. Apparently, a third person had been arrested in connection with the raid. Since three guys left together, that meant Quint was in jail.

This wasn't the worst-case scenario that had been running through Ree's head, because it meant he was still alive. She wouldn't exactly celebrate, though, because it also meant Quint had to pull out of the hunt for justice for Tessa. Dumitru and his people wouldn't have anything to do with Quint now. The fact he was released from jail would signal to them that he must have given up information in return for a plea deal.

On the one hand, relief washed over Ree that the case was coming to a close.

However, for Quint's sanity, she wished he'd gotten the closure he needed in order to put Tessa and her baby's deaths behind him. This way, he would always be haunted. It was a no-win situation now.

The thought of not seeing Quint when she entered the apartment weighed heavily on her mind. She wanted to see he was safe and alive with her own two eyes. *It was over*, she repeated.

Their apartment was no longer needed. Ree would go inside, take a shower and pack up her few belongings. She didn't want to leave Dallas without Quint, so she planned to stick around until his release. They could brief another team and let someone else find a way in. Quint wasn't the only one who wanted justice for Tessa.

Walking into their building, the weight on her chest pressed harder. The elevator ride was short this time. She slowly took her key out of her purse. The minute she unlocked the door, it opened.

Ree's heart took a hit at seeing Quint standing there. He quickly ushered her inside, closed the door behind her before engaging the lock, and then hauled her against his chest.

"What? How?" She blinked a couple of times, unable to trust her own eyes as she looped her arms around his neck and ran her fingers through the back of his hair. The move caused her breasts to press against a brick-wall chest.

"I'm here."

"Who is in jail then?" she asked. "Giselle said a third person has been arrested."

"A stand-in who has my ID and is being paid well for

an acting job," he stated. "I just got word on the raid at Vadik's penthouse. He's been arrested, too."

"How?" she asked, amazed by his quick thinking.

"I'd rather kiss you than answer work questions right now," he stated a moment before her lips found his.

Their mouths moved together in a perfect dance. Her pulse climbed as something as simple as taking in air suddenly became less of a priority. Her head swam in the fog that was Quint Casey and she realized in that moment just how lost she was in his arms. Lost in the best possible way. In a way that made her want to stay there longer and just be.

When she pulled back, she admitted, "I love you, Quint. That might be too fast and I have no idea if you're ready to hear it, but wondering if something had happened to you made me realize just how important you are to me."

His arms tightened around her. Her body was flush with his. He leaned down as his lips almost grazed her ear. He whispered, "I love you, Ree. I've been wanting to say those words for days without knowing how or if you wanted to hear them after the way I showed up at your house."

This time, their kisses were tender, loving and long.

"There's no question I'm in love with you, Quint." She pulled back enough to catch his gaze and hold on to it. "What do we do about it?"

"I don't need a trial run," he started. "All I need is a U-Haul truck and space cleared out at your place for a few of my things. I want to move in together, Ree." He got down on one knee. "And I want you to marry me."

When he looked up at her, tears filled her eyes and her heart detonated.

"Marriage is a big step, Quint," she said, barely able to take in enough air to fill her lungs.

"Are you scared? We can wait. *I* can wait," he said.

"We've waited long enough," she stated with a certainty she'd never known. "I'm in love with you and I want to spend the rest of our lives together."

"Does that mean I can bring my U-Haul?" he asked with a smile that melted all of her resolve.

"It means I'll go with you to pick it up," she said, tugging him to his feet. "But I have one condition."

"Name it," he said without hesitation.

"I want a puppy," she said, unable to stop smiling. Quint was here. He was hers. And they were pledging to spend the rest of their lives together.

"As long as you say yes to marrying me you can have anything you want," he said with a smile.

"Yes," she said. "I'll marry you, Quint Casey. I'll be your wife. Your real wife."

Quint stood up and claimed her lips one more time. This time, Ree knew she'd found home.

BAGS WERE PACKED at Quint's place, and he was about to turn out the lights at the apartment before heading to Ree's house. *Their* house, he corrected. Quint needed to get used to the idea because Ree was the best thing that had ever happened to him and there was no way he was letting her get away after she'd said she loved him. He'd been searching for the right way to tell her the same thing.

Axel had been reunited with his family and sent to a long-term safehouse. Someone was heading over to pick up Giselle and offer WITSEC. And the girls Vadik and his crew were trafficking had been reunited with their families. Their trauma was unthinkable and healing would take time. But every single one of them was home, safe in their own beds.

"Let me get this straight. Someone is posing as you in jail right now and Bjorn is working out the details," Ree stated as they stood at the door.

"That's right," Quint confirmed. "The case is dead, so there's no reason for me to stick around any longer."

"I'm sorry, Quint. I know how important it is to you to be the one to bring Dumitru down," Ree said.

"As long as he goes down, I'll be happy," he said, but they both knew that wasn't entirely true. He'd wanted to be the one to slap cuffs on the bastard responsible. And now, would Dumitru ever trust Quint enough to get anywhere near him?

His cell buzzed. Quint checked the screen.

Get rid of Vadik. Come see me when it's done and you're out. Dumitru

The text from Agent Grappell shocked Quint. The desk agent explained this message had been written in a note handed to Quint's stand-in by a prison guard.

The message would need to be authenticated before a plan could be developed, but this meant he was still in the game.

"What is it?" Ree asked as another text came in.

Quint checked the screen to find another message from Grappell. If Quint was moving up to work with Dumitru, the offer to Giselle needed to be put on hold.

"Nothing. I'll tell you in the car," he said. Now, he just had to figure out a way to tell his bride-to-be this wasn't over. At least, not for him.

* * * * *

Look for the conclusion of A Ree and Quint Novel series by USA TODAY *bestselling author Barb Han when* Mission Honeymoon *goes on sale next month!*

And if you missed the previous books in the series, you can find Undercover Couple *and* Newlywed Assignment *now, wherever Harlequin Intrigue books are sold!*

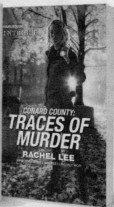

COMING NEXT MONTH FROM

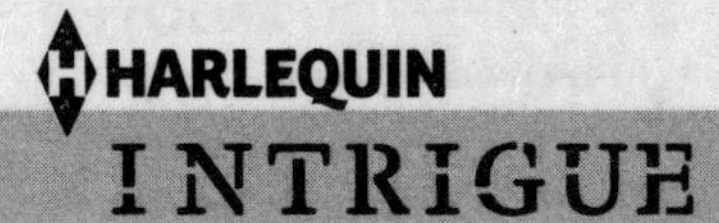

#2085 MAVERICK JUSTICE

The Law in Lubbock County • by Delores Fossen

Fleeing the hospital—and a deadly threat—Delaney Archer runs to Cash Mercer, the one man she trusts. Except the Clay Ridge sheriff and rancher hasn't seen the public defender in a year, not since Delaney ended their engagement. Can the Texas lawman shield her from a desperate killer... and the explosive truth?

#2086 SCENT DETECTION

K-9s on Patrol • by Leslie Marshman

Veterinarian Marie Beaumont's spent five years in witness protection hiding from a ruthless foe—until she and her K-9 save a handsome stranger with amnesia, who begins to remember her as the woman she once was. But is Jack a caring, electrifying protector...or a killer sent to finish off Marie, once and for all?

#2087 MISSION HONEYMOON

A Ree and Quint Novel • by Barb Han

Rule-breaking ATF agent Quint Casey is *this* close to nailing the ruthless weapons kingpin who murdered his first partner. But he and his undercover wife, Agent Ree Sheppard, are running a gauntlet of unexpected traps—and their wild-card irresistible passion for each other is putting everything at risk...

#2088 LAKESIDE MYSTERY

The Lost Girls • by Carol Ericson

LAPD detective Denver Holt doesn't know what to make of true crime blogger Ashlynn Hughes—but she has inside information that can help him crack his biggest homicide case yet. As anonymous tips carry them further into danger, Denver wonders if he can keep a target off Ashlynn's back...or if she'll be silenced for good.

#2089 SHIELDING HER SON

West Investigations • by K.D. Richards

Erika Powell has lived in hiding for years to protect her son from his wealthy, tyrannical grandfather. But when attempts are made on Erika's life, neighbor James West fears he may have endangered her—because the undercover PI's investigation of Erika might have led someone dangerous right to her.

#2090 REVENGE ON THE RANCH

Kings of Coyote Creek • by Carla Cassidy

The attack that lands Luke King in the hospital won't stop the Kansas rancher from bringing his father's murderer to justice. But when Carrie Carlson, the nurse who offers to join forces with him, narrowly misses being shot, can Luke fulfill his dangerous quest and keep her from the clutches of a vengeful killer?

SPECIAL EXCERPT FROM

HARLEQUIN

INTRIGUE

ATF agents Ree Sheppard and Quint Casey are closing in on the criminal at the center of a weapons smuggling ring they've been investigating while working undercover. But once the bad guys are behind bars, will Ree and Quint be able to transition their fake marriage to the real-life relationship they're both craving?

Keep reading for a sneak peek at
Mission Honeymoon,
the final book in USA TODAY *bestselling author Barb Han's A Ree and Quint Novel series.*

His hands cupped her face. She blinked up at him.

"They buried me," she said, fighting the emotion trying to take over at the thought of never seeing him again.

Anger flashed in his blue eyes, and his jaw muscles clenched. "They better never touch you again. We can make an excuse to get you out of here. Say one of your family members is sick and you had to go."

"They'll see it as weakness," she reminded him. "It'll hurt the case."

He thumbed a loose tendril of hair off her face.

"I don't care, Ree," he said with an overwhelming intensity that became its own physical presence. "I can't lose you."

Those words hit her with the force of a tsunami.

HIEXP0622

Neither of them could predict what would happen next. Neither could guarantee this case wouldn't go south. Neither could guarantee they would both walk away in one piece.

"Let's take ourselves off the case together," she said, knowing full well he wouldn't take her up on the offer but suggesting it anyway.

Quint didn't respond. When she pulled back and looked into his eyes, she understood why. A storm brewed behind those sapphire-blues, crystalizing them, sending fiery streaks to contrast against the whites. Those babies were the equivalent of a raging wildfire that would be impossible to put out or contain. People said eyes were the window to the soul. In Quint's case, they seemed the window to his heart.

He pressed his forehead against hers and took in an audible breath. When he exhaled, it was like he was releasing all his pent-up frustration and fear. In that moment, she understood the gravity of what he'd been going through while she'd been gone. Kidnapped. For all he knew, left for dead.

So she didn't speak, either. Instead, she leaned into their connection, a connection that tethered them as an electrical current ran through her to him and back. For a split second, it was impossible to determine where he ended and she began.

HARLEQUIN